The Barn that Crowed

Anne Davey Koomans

This book is dedicated to my dear friend:

Joyce Arlene Comer
June 30, 1928 – July 24, 2020

When God told me I should write a series of nine books, Joyce motivated me to write this series of books for young readers. She suggested I write books for children from eight to the mid-teens.

She and I discussed names and dates for the books. We both fondly remembered 1946, the year after World War II had ended. It was a marvelous time for Joyce, America, and me. Families loved family members, the USA, and especially God.

Joyce asked that I name one of the leading characters Joyce and her mother Iris Belle, after her mother.

Joyce told me that she and her husband took one of their daughters with them to the Bahamas for a business meeting. They noticed their daughter came back with a lot more confidence. She had played a game on the pin ball machine in the building at the boarding dock for the ship. She won and those watching told her she was great. I created a chapter from that information, and Joyce approved it. The book was started.

SPECIAL THANK YOU'S TO:

GOD – Thank you God for telling me to write the nine books.

Roberta Gotham – Thank you Roberta for critiquing and editing the book.

Camille St. Clair – Thank you Camille for critiquing and reviewing the book.

Lois Hettinger – Thank you Lois for reading and reviewing the book.

Ellen Copeland – Thank you Ellen for reading and reviewing the book.

Sara Emma Pineiros – Thank you Emma for reading and reviewing the book.

Diana Mendez – Thank you Diana, and Author Creatives staff, for all your help, expertise, and patience needed to get this book published. God bless!

Ellis Sandlin – Ellis is a singer and guitar player who lives in my Senior complex. He entertains the residents with concerts; and plays and leads the music for our monthly sing-alongs. He has given me written permission to use his name in the nine books.

Contents

1   A Saturday with Friends. 1

2   Introduction of the Martin Family. 13

3   Meeting the Perkins 17

4   Preparing for a Brave Adventure 20

5   Birds. 24

6   Gaining the Courage to Enter the Barn 28

7   Railroad Tracks 32

8   Roosters, Roosters, but who else lives in the barn?. . . 35

9   Mr. Spitznaugle to the Rescue. 37

10   The History of the Barn. 41

11   Elevators are Important to Merrysville 48

12   Who Invented the Ponds? 52

13   We Need history. 59

14   The Barn that Crows 63

15   Tennis Anyone? 72

16   A Different Summer 77

17   Summer has Begun 85

18   Plans for Decoration Day. 98

19   Good Deed for May. 110

20   And Life Goes On 149

21   Welcome to Merrysville 152

22   Time to Plan the Fun. 160

23   After the Party 166

"INTRODUCTION TO THE BARN"

Chapter One

A Saturday with Friends

Jimmy was often asked by Amanda if she and Joyce could go with him and his friends on their next adventure. He really enjoyed having her around but, being an older brother, he didn't want her to know how much. On Friday evening, Amanda asked Jimmy if she, Joyce, and some of their girlfriends could join the boys on their Saturday morning adventures. He told her, "You can come if you don't scream when the roosters are crowing." She simply said, "OK."

Betty Martin pointed out to her two children, "Tomorrow will be May 4th, which means you children have only twelve days before school is out for the summer. Jimmy, I feel that Amanda, Joyce, and their girlfriends will have fun if they go with you and your friends. With summer coming up, it may be the last time that all of you will be available to go on an adventure together."

Amanda and her best friend Joyce knew that their brothers Jimmy and Bob were as afraid as the girls were of getting near those ugly roosters who lived in that spooky barn.

Amanda and two girlfriends knocked on Joyce's door at eight forty-five on Saturday morning. Joyce quickly opened the door and invited the girls in to have some homemade cinnamon rolls and milk. Her brother came around the corner and asked, "Where are Jimmy and the other four boys? Aren't they coming?" Amanda assured Bob that the boys were waiting for Jason Hanaway, and they would be right over.

No sooner said than the boys were noisily coming up onto the porch. They were trying to stomp the mud and water off their shoes, and onto the mat. They finally took off their muddy shoes and walked to the door in their stockinged feet. As soon as Bob opened the door, the boys came in and sat down on chairs or the floor. They were soon eating some of the hot, delicious cinnamon rolls that Iris Belle had just removed from the oven. Bob opened another gallon of milk and poured it into the glasses.

As everyone was finishing their cinnamon rolls and milk, Bob said, "The sky has finally cleared up after that big rain and an hour of threatening drizzle. How about going over to the park and taking that one trail that we have always been curious about where it goes?" A quiet gasp went around the table. Wiping their smiling faces with their napkins, all nine of the kids nodded enthusiastically in agreement with Bob's plan.

Joyce and Amanda had made their plans too. Before they went to bed, the girls talked to their mothers about cooking hamburgers with mushrooms and onions for dinner on Saturday if they were able to find mushrooms to pick when they were with their brothers and girlfriends. Both mothers were pleased with the suggestion. Amanda's mother felt positive that there were many mushrooms across the railroad tracks, about one hundred feet west from the park. "The morels in that area grow big, especially around the rotted tree stumps, sticks, and limbs, by the small woods. You and Jimmy know the good ones that can be eaten. There is also an area near there where poisonous ones grow, so do not let anyone touch those. Today is May 3rd. Last year your dads found many in that area on May 1st. You may remember that we had hamburgers with mushrooms and onions that day."

Early on Saturday morning, the girls had chosen two large baskets with strong handles. They filled them with lots of empty quart-size cardboard containers for everyone to pick fresh mushrooms, if they got near the railroad tracks. They remembered last year when they were walking down the tracks in June, they discovered ripe strawberries and raspberries. They had made themselves sick eating so many because they did not have a container to carry some home. Amanda and Joyce declared at that time to always have something with them to bring home any edible treasures they found on their excursions.

Bob wanted to surprise his sister and friends so he and his mother had made ten peanut butter sandwiches for him to carry in his knapsack.

He was in for a surprise himself when he later opened his knapsack and discovered his generous mother had wrapped ten large sugar cookies in waxed papers for the kids. Bob was in bed when she slipped them into his knapsack. Bob's mom and dad had to giggle when they thought about the look of surprise that was going to be on Bob's face.

As the boys and girls rounded the corner a block from the barn, they were spotted by the roosters. Their noisy, sharp "Cock-a-doodle-doo! Cock-a-doodle-doo!" could be heard a block away. The Martin and Perkins parents smiled as they were having their second cup of coffee.

The roosters caught the boys off guard and one of them slipped on the wet pavement. His hands and blue jeans were a muddy mess. Jimmy helped him up. He couldn't help but smile when he saw the black streak across his friend's nose, cheek, and hair. None of the children said anything.

Jason pointed to the row of tall pine trees near the water. The kids spotted several nests, protected by overhanging bushes and trees. The mother ducks sat, keeping the eggs warm while the drakes sat in the grass, keeping guard over the mothers on the nests.

The duck sitting on the first nest stood up and revealed that she was sitting on many eggs, none hatched.

When they were near the second nest, the mother duck reached out her beak in a disgusted manner, barely missing Bob's hand, as she was trying to bite him. The drake sitting nearby, stood up, spread his wings in warning, and chased all the kids away from the nests under the pine tree that the ducks claimed as their roof.

When they came to a third nest under another tree, Amanda squealed with delight as the mother duck stood up and revealed the six young ducklings in her nest. All the children knew that they were not to disturb the nests, so they went on to their next adventure.

The water looked so warm that a few of the kids took off their shoes and socks to test the water.

Several frogs sat on a log by the water's edge. Each boy scooped up a frog and was chasing the girls. Although the girls sounded like they were scared to death as they were running and screaming, it was only yesterday when Amanda and Joyce were holding those same frogs. A snapping turtle swam to the log just then and proceeded to scare away the remaining frogs who were soaking up the sun that just began to shine.

The turtle snapped at one of the boy's pant legs, and the frogs were quickly dropped into the water. Amanda's secret was that this turtle was known as Tootsie, the nickname given to her by Amanda on her frequent visits to the sunning branch used by many snapping turtles. One of the girls shouted, "Amanda, I believe that turtle looked at you like it knew you." Jimmy snorted, "Fat chance!" Amanda said nothing aloud.

The next stop was going to be the fishing spot around the large pond. The boys had their favorite fishing poles hidden there under their favorite tree. The girls didn't have any fishing gear so they told the boys they would say goodbye and head to the playground area.

Unbeknown to anyone but Joyce, Amanda couldn't stand to put a worm on the hook. She didn't want the boys to know that secret. Joyce could hook the worms as well as any of the boys could. She always took care of Amanda's line when the girls fished alone. Once Amanda caught a whopper. It was huge and heavy. The girls believed it probably was the largest fish in the ponds. They never told the boys, but they often had caught some nice size fish, but thrown them back before going home.

Both of their mothers had told them last year to let the boys be the fishing heroes. The girls were smart; they took their mothers' advice; it had worked out all right. They did not want to appear too competitive to their brothers in all areas. After all, being the best at fishing was the utmost goal of all the boys. They never seemed to have time to waste exercising.

For the next hour or so, the girls had fun chatting on the swings. With exercise equipment next to the swings, the girls felt compelled to do a few pull-ups and push-ups. The sun's temperature was beginning to heat the day. After checking to verify that other baby ducklings had hatched, and some were already swimming in the water with their mothers, the girls returned to the pond.

The boys were disgusted and declared that it was because of last night's rain that none of them had caught even one fish. Bob said, "Hey girls, why don't we go do something else? We can fish again after we're done with our adventure." Everyone agreed.

Next to the railroad track, about twenty feet down from the edge of the park, was a large overhead water tower. It had a huge pipe for the train driver to put water into the train's storage tanks for steam, drinking, and the bathrooms.

Every kid had loved watching the trains when they slowed down to fill their train with the water they needed. The procedure looked so easy when it was done by the train employee. One of Jimmy's friends said, "Let's go see how that thing works." Everyone followed him because they were as curious as he was.

Jimmy noticed the long chain on the water tower. He figured it was used by the train driver to pull the water down into the train storage tanks. Since he was twelve-years old, the tallest, and the bravest, he grabbed the chain and, in the middle of a wide swing, was nearly drowned when a twenty-six-inch-wide spout of water knocked him and Jason to the ground. The other boys started to laugh but soon learned it was no laughing matter. The other three boys pulled down on the thick chain. With all the boys working, they had a hard time getting the water shut off.

Everyone got squirted by the water before it shut off. Jimmy took hours to dry off. Bob had his friend remove his shirt and t-shirt. He squeezed out a lot of water from the shirt and t-shirt while Jimmy was finally able to stand up. He was shaking from the shock of the powerful cold water. Bob asked him if he wanted to go back home, but he wanted to go on. Bob took off his own tee shirt and gave it to Jimmy so he wouldn't catch a cold. It was warm enough that Bob felt comfortable in his shirt. Jimmy found a sturdy stick to carry and hung his shirts on it. He laughed and said he felt like a hobo. The kids all giggled and told him they could see a resemblance.

Bob was marking many landmarks with the white chalk. He said his dad had told him to do that so if he and Joyce were ever late getting home, he could follow the chalk landmarks to find them.

The land along the railroad tracks was full of green wild strawberries and raspberries that would be delicious in June and July. Amanda reminded her friends, "Mother told Dad that it will be at least four weeks before the raspberries near the tracks will ripen, but someone told her that the strawberries should be ripe and delicious in three weeks. Mushrooms are already at their peak." Knowing that helped them make the decision on which way to go.

Jason's stomach growled and everyone asked if he could be hungry since he had eaten so many cinnamon rolls. He pointed up to the sun and said, "Yes, I am hungry. The sun looks like it's past noon, maybe even one o'clock. I guess we'll have to go back home. That water tower took a long time out of our fun."

Bob said, "Not to worry." He took the peanut butter sandwiches out of his knapsack and passed them around, one-by-one. Everyone was pleased to sit right down on the metal railroad track and eat their sandwich. Bob was shocked when he discovered the ten cookies wrapped in wax paper in his knapsack. Everyone cheered. They told Bob and Joyce to thank their mother for such a great and delicious surprise.

They agreed to walk down the tracks to gather the mushrooms. Jimmy and Bob were thinking that they would also gather strawberries when they came this way in three weeks. Everyone was amazed at the abundant number of mushrooms sitting in clusters.

Before they had finished picking the mushrooms, they were surprised by the loud, shrill train whistle of a passenger train passing White's Crossing. The kids soon smiled and waved at passengers of the twelve-car train. The train driver blew his whistle again and waved at the children as the train swiftly passed the mushroom field where the kids would soon finish picking mushrooms.

What an unexpected surprise for the passengers to see ten boys and girls waving and holding up quart boxes of freshly picked mushrooms by a nearby woods, in the Indiana countryside.

Chris whistled and said, "Wow!! That was a surprise. I've never been so close to a train going that fast. I guess they must slow down when they go past the crossings in Merrysville." Bob said, "I was thinking the same thing."

All containers were full when they came to a shallow, narrow creek under the railroad tracks. Everyone took off their shoes and socks and started walking on the ground, down toward the middle of the water.

Jimmy warned everyone, "I've got a feeling that it will not be easy walking on the rocks in this creek. Here we are holding our mushrooms in one hand and shoes and socks in the other." Bob spoke up, "But it's going to be so much fun that it will be worth the challenge."

Even though it had rained, the water was warm and probably no more than twelve inches deep. The rocks turned out to be so smooth from the water flowing over them for years that they felt like velvet to the kids' feet.

After about fifty feet, the creek bank was no longer ground level, and the girls noticed that the creek had quickly gone downhill. Some of the boys began racing ahead. Suddenly Amanda noticed those boys were up on the ground above the creek, screaming for everyone to get out of the water.

The bank suddenly seemed high from where Joyce, Amanda, and their girlfriends stood in the water. They raised their hands and had the boys help pull them out of the creek, and onto the tall grass where the boys stood. They saw the other boys and girls looking into the creek, obviously concerned about something in the water. One girlfriend nearly screamed, "Look! look!" Joyce answered, "What are you looking at?"

All the boys were talking at the same time. Finally, Jimmy was able to answer, "Look for yourself." When the kids looked down at the side of the creek bank, they noticed many holes like those they had passed along the bank. They were horrified to see that the holes were now occupied by snakes that had come out to see who was invading their territory.

Bob nearly screamed, "Doggone it! Why were you guys in such a hurry? When you were running so hard and fast, the earth must have shaken where the snakes' nests are. They came out to defend themselves." When the kids heard the loud "rattle, rattle", Jimmy screamed, "Oh no! Rattlesnakes! They're poisonous!"

All the kids ran as fast as they could, away from the creek, and onto the gravel road. Those rocks were not smooth. One little boy lost most of his mushrooms, but no one stopped to pick them up. No one stopped to put their socks and shoes onto their dusty, dirty, and sore feet, until they had run nearly a thousand feet. The children never went down into the water of that creek again, nor did they ever remember to tell their parents about their experience on that adventure.

Chapter Two

Introduction of the Martin Family

A manda Martin was a very smart ten-year-old tomboy, who loved wearing hand-me-downs from her twelve-year-old brother, Jimmy. She seldom wore girls' blouses, skirts, or dresses. Amanda didn't like to wear shoes at all, but being a tomboy, her busy activities required that she wear them. She went barefoot anytime she could. Amanda loved to talk and was not a bit shy. The school considered Amanda the smartest student in their school system. She just finished the fifth grade but attended math and English classes with students in the high school.

Amanda and her brother, Jimmy, both had red hair like their dad, John. Both children disliked the freckles that seemed to belong to every kid with red hair. Apparently, their dad had outgrown his freckles, so Amanda and Jimmy looked forward to the day when they would lose theirs. Most people commented on their lovely brown eyes, and did not even notice their hair or freckles, but that was the only thing the kids saw when they looked in a mirror. Because Amanda was always smiling and laughing, everyone considered her beautiful, often comparing her to her lovely mother, Betty.

Amanda was the tallest girl in her class. Other than her brother Jimmy, she could run the fastest of anyone in elementary and junior high school, as well as many high school students. She also could do the most pull-ups and push-ups of anyone in the school. All the boys chose her first to be on their baseball team during recess. Amanda was chosen because she hit the most home runs, but she would only play on the team that would agree to choose Joyce. She had many playmates, but her best friend was definitely Joyce Perkins.

Joyce called her Amanda, but some of her other friends called her "String Bean". She didn't care.

Amanda liked short hair because she sweated a lot when she was running. When she would sweat, her red ringlets used to fall apart, and her hair would look straggly after she played for a short while.

When she was eight, her mother finally cut Amanda's hair short and styled it in a cute, layered look. Amanda's natural curl kept her short hair from getting stringy. Her hair looked like it was two shades of red and was always shiny.

Amanda's twelve-year-old brother, Jimmy, was tall too, and like Amanda, looked like he hadn't eaten for a long time. Most of his seventh-grade friends used the nickname "Beanpole" for Jimmy. Most people, who did not know him, thought he was at least fourteen because he was so tall. Jimmy's dad, John Martin, used a bowl to cut Jimmy's red hair. The bowl cut was popular in 1946 for boys in grade school and Junior High.

Their family could never understand why both kids were so slim. Jimmy and Amanda loved food, especially the yummy cooking and baking of their mother. All their friends loved coming to their house after school because of the homemade cookies and cinnamon rolls that Betty often served with ice-cold milk.

Jimmy sometimes seemed a little clumsy because he was growing taller every day. He often ran faster than was safe with his lack of leg coordination. Today as usual, his arms and legs seemed to have bruises and scars on them. In fact, both his right knee and left elbow appeared to have fresh stitches on them. His hand still had a scar from his fall two weeks ago.

Amanda always cried whenever she saw blood from one of her rare scrapes, but even as a little boy, Jimmy had always tried to be brave, and never cry, even when he was hurt badly.

The Martin Gardens was a well-known company in Indiana. Their dad, John Martin, raised vegetables, fruit, and honeybees.

They had hundreds of acres of vegetables. Their fruit orchards were full of apple, peach, pear, and apricot trees, strawberries, grapes, and black raspberries.

Many local women worked for Betty Martin on part-time schedules. Those women raised acres of vibrant flowers and baked delicious cookies and pies. They also produced colorful aprons and kitchen linens in Betty's Sewing Room. Betty had many customers who came to her house to buy her hand-crafted items, flowers, cookies, and pies.

Most of the items from her Sewing Room were sold in specialty shops in nearby cities. The Martin Gardens sold produce and other items to national chain grocery stores, area restaurants, and even in a local farmers' market.

On the edge of town, on the other side of one of his large storage barns, were one hundred hives of honeybees. Many were four or five supers high. The bees were located there to make the orchard blossoms become fruit. John loved working with bees, and taught Bee Keeping to local 4-H students.

Betty had a plum tree that was just for her family. It grew in the family backyard. Her plum butter and plum jelly were the best that anyone had ever tasted. Many people wanted to buy several jars, but Betty let them know the plum tree was only for her family.

Their children learned the responsibilities involved in growing vegetables and fruit. They were paid twenty-five cents an hour for picking and cleaning vegetables and fruit. The children also learned how to manage money. In the summer, John hired many of the children who lived in the village.

Amanda's mother, Betty, was a great listener who gave the children sound advice and allowed them the freedom to develop their talents. She remembered being a tomboy when she was Amanda's age, so she loved the experience of reliving her youth with Amanda's many adventures.

Chapter Three

Meeting the Perkins

J oyce Perkins was a beautiful, petite, ten-year-old blonde girl with long ringlets that always kept their shape. Her hair had not been cut for six years. She had gorgeous blue eyes, like her beautiful mother, Iris Belle Perkins. Joyce had a twin brother, Bob. They had just finished the fifth grade. Bob had hazel eyes like his dad, Art Perkins.

Whenever Joyce was near older women, they seemed to feel compelled to squeeze her lovely round cheeks. She never seemed to mind. Joyce's face wore the most gorgeous dimples you can imagine. She always wrinkled her cute nose when she was scared, frustrated or angry, which was not very often. Amanda always noticed when she did this.

Because of her clothes, posture, and perfect hair, many people asked Iris Belle if Joyce was a model. Because Joyce felt shy around most people, Iris Belle knew modeling by Joyce would never happen. Joyce never felt shy when she was around her best friend Amanda Martin.

Joyce always looked dressed up in the skirts and blouses or ruffled dresses that she wore, not only to school and to church, but also for play. Her rich grandmother always made sure that Joyce had matching socks for every dress she bought for her.

While Joyce was always the shortest girl in her class, Bob was almost as tall as his friend Jimmy Martin. No one could believe Joyce and Bob were twins.

Bob's socks always looked like they were drooping and falling into his shoes. It seemed to Joyce that Bob was always leaning over, pulling up his socks. She liked to tease him about it. His dimples seemed deeper when he was embarrassed. No droopy socks for Joyce.

Bob Perkins' best friend was Jimmy Martin, his next-door neighbor. Bob weighed about twenty-five pounds more than Jimmy, although Jimmy was taller and two years older than Bob. Both boys had seen the other one cry a few times when they were hurt, but they never teased each other, nor told anyone else.

Bob loved wearing shorts because he was a lot like Jimmy. He loved to run everywhere, and when he wore long pants, he often tore the pant legs on a rock, fence, or some other obstacle. Whenever a pant leg was torn, he was happy to have his mother cut the pant legs into shorts.

Joyce and Bob's dad, Art Perkins, was a successful commercial real estate salesman. He also sold commercial insurance and had several other businesses that provided his family with a comfortable income.

You would have to call Iris Belle just a little plump, but no one noticed because of those blue eyes and fantastic smile. Iris Belle was best known for entertaining, and her large collection of aprons - - some long, some short. Unless she went shopping or to church, you always saw her wearing one of them. When she made a dress, she always made a matching apron to wear with it. She was the best-dressed woman in town.

Iris Belle's parents were quite rich. Joyce and Bob's mother, her brother and sister had grown up in a large home, near Indianapolis, only sixty miles away.

During the depression, their grandparents' business had survived, and flourished after the Second World War began. Their rich grandmother loved to buy clothes for Joyce and Bob from an expensive children's store. Bob loved his grandma, but not her choice of clothes for him.

Chapter Four

Preparing for a Brave Adventure

"**C**ock-a-doodle-doo! Cock-a-doodle-doo!"
Amanda Martin and her brother Jimmy smiled across the breakfast table at their friends Joyce and Bob Perkins. Amanda turned toward Joyce and said, "Did you hear that? I know it was faint, but that was those chickens crowing. I can hardly wait to see inside their barn." Joyce smiled and joined the boys with, "Me too."

They all laughed and the four of them were talking and eating as fast as they could. Betty Martin, Amanda and Jimmy's mother, was busily placing the last of the pancakes on the platter.

When the noise from the roosters quieted down, a different sound could be heard, coming through the window by the table. Many birds that returned to Merrysville, Indiana, from the south in the last few weeks were already awake and chirping. Betty looked out the window. Both three-tier birdfeeders were crowded with birds of various colors. The two Killdeer were the first to arrive in Indiana and had already elected to build their nest on the yard under low, thick bushes. Betty thought to herself that there would be eggs in that nest in the next week or two. She was surprised to see two Snipes and three Nuthatches near the fence.

The yard was ablaze with flowering trees and lilac bushes. Betty took a deep breath of the wonderful aroma. Crocuses were visible but fading. Violets were a deeper purple this year. Daffodils seemed a brighter yellow. Tulips were popping up or blooming in every flower bed.

Betty smiled as she opened the window a little higher and asked the kids what bird they could identify by their special voices. Each of the kids looked toward the open window and concentrated on listening to the many different sounds. They could tell that some of the birds were in their trees and others sounded like they were a block away.

One by one Betty heard about the following birds: Crows cawing over a dead animal, the Mourning Dove's plaintive call, the loud hooting of the Owl in the large oak tree in the side yard, and the list went on and on. Betty told them, "You're right. I can hear every bird you mentioned. Take a quick look outside. The yard is full of Robins pulling up the worms. The rain last night helped their effort. The fog is still near the ground. I wonder if that helps them hear the worms moving underground." The four kids all said, "Maybe," but seemed surprised at something else they saw. Jimmy whistled and said,

"Wow! Look! The fog is really thick." As Bob glanced up at the wall clock, he smiled, turned toward Jimmy, and said, "Just six more minutes and the boys should be here."

Betty Martin placed the platter on the table and poured milk.

When the children had finished breakfast, they put their dirty dishes in the dishwater in the sink, and quickly went into the bathroom to wash their hands. Betty was finishing the dishes when the doorbell rang. Betty looked at the clock and said to herself, "Six-thirty a.m., right on time." Two smiling, enthusiastic boys stood near the door. One looked at the empty table and quickly asked, "Are Bob and Jimmy awake?"

Betty smiled as she nodded and invited them in. She looked toward the hallway and announced, "Your friends are here."

The children were smiling when they returned to the dining room, with a cheerful, "Hi Jason and Chris, are you ready to go?" Chris had a big smile on his face as he declared, "We're ready. Mrs. Martin today is a great day, May 17th; the day after school was let out for the summer. Just think, no school today. This is the first Friday we have been able to plan adventures and fishing. We know that this year, 1946, is going to be the best year of our lives." Betty loved his attitude and told him, "I think you are right."

Once more "Cock-a-doodle-doo! Cock-a-doodle-doo!"- faintly echoed throughout the room. All six children smiled, clapped their hands, and declared, "Oh yeh! It's time. Let's go." As four children quickly thanked her for breakfast, Betty could see that everyone was anxious to get started on something that was going to be a fun adventure.

Betty stood near the door and asked the children, "What are the six of you planning to do so early in the morning? As soon as the fog lifts, it's going to be beautiful; the sun should be shining through the fog within an hour." Having already opened the door, Jimmy quickly explained that they were going on an exploration of the big barn over at the park. "We want to see where those chickens live."

Betty quickly advised the children, "That barn is the private property of Mr. Andy Spitznaugle. I have never been in there. If there is a sign inviting people to tour the barn, I guess you can go in. If there is a sign that says, 'No Trespassing,' promise me that you will not enter."

Betty moved aside as she agreed that their plans sounded like a fun thing to do. With the door open, the "Cock-a-doodle-doo! Cock-a-doodle-doo!" seemed louder. The children were already running when Betty shouted, "By the way, those are roosters, not chickens." She left the room smiling on her way to dry and put away the dishes.

Chapter Five

Birds

Betty Martin had sparked an interest in the children to be aware of different birds and their sounds. At school, only five or six weeks ago, the children spent more than two weeks learning all about local birds and others from around the world. The six kids looked all around, searching for the sight of birds in the many trees on both sides of the street.

All the kids were used to watching birds eating from their family bird feeders. In their yard, they had just seen first-hand many of the Robins that came back three weeks ago. "Look!" Chris shouted. He pointed to two Blue Jays that were nearly hidden on a limb in a tall pine tree. In the same tree, the girls spotted a pair of red Cardinals. The kids discussed how much brighter red and more beautiful the male was than the female.

When the kids all looked up at the telephone wire crossing the street, it was full of birds. There were eight beautiful Red-winged Blackbirds in a row; further down were many Pigeons; Sparrows sat in a row; and looking very lonely, was a single Sea Gull. Even though the air was foggy, the shiny black coats of the Blackbirds looked like silk. The kids wondered if the loud chatter coming from the Blackbirds was a private communication, or a greeting to the boys and girls. They smiled as they waved at all the beautiful birds and yelled, "Good morning birds!"

When Bob asked if a bird, barely visible in an elm tree, was a White-Eye, everyone laughed. Chris reminded Bob that they learned in school that the White-Eye lives in Africa and the Pacific area. However, no one recognized the greenish-colored bird with white around its eyes that was staring at them. It looked so much like the picture the teacher showed them last month of the White-Eye. Bob quickly reminded his friends that their teacher had told them of other birds that migrated north in the last few years when they had warmer winters than normal.

Jason reminded him that the teacher had said the White-Eye probably would never get this far north. No one said anything but, like Bob, everyone was wondering, "Could it be? No, I don't think so. No, it can't be, not from that far away, but it sure looks like a White-Eye."

Everyone saw several species of Sparrows flying in all directions. They seemed to be busy that morning. Jimmy spotted his first Whippoorwill for the year. He had never seen one during the day. He figured it was out in the daytime because the fog made the night seem longer. The Whippoorwill was running, zigzagging through the brush, headed for its nest where it would spend the day sleeping. Joyce laughed and told Jimmy, "That's a hard bird to spell." Everyone laughed as they tried to get a look at it before it disappeared.

The kids separated the weeds and brush to watch closely. Before it arrived at its nest, the Whippoorwill surprised a Grouse and a Titmouse who were in the brush. They seemed to be in a frenzy and ran out into the open, near the children. It shocked both birds as much as it did the children.

The boys went toward the brush to see what else was in there. To their surprise, there were several Titmice eating something off the ground; they didn't leave their breakfast but kept eating. Amanda pointed to Pheasants and nesting Ducks just a few feet away.

Suddenly, three black Crows seemed to come out of nowhere to follow the loud "Caw, Caw" on the side road that the children were about to pass. Bob said he thought these might be the birds they had heard in the Martin dining room. There were two other Crows sitting in the middle of the street, picking at a dead rabbit that had been run over. All five Crows were competing for their breakfast.

The girls nearly cried and the boys voiced remorse for the rabbit, but Joyce quickly reminded her friends about their science teacher telling the class that rabbits and mice were in God's food chain for many other animals. Their science book explained that food animals multiplied more quickly than most.

Jason reminded everyone that they had also learned at school that Crows are an important part of God's and nature's way to keep the environment free of many possible diseases.

The rat-a-tat-tat in a tree on the left side of the road made them all stop and look at the biggest red headed Woodpecker any of the children had ever seen. It looked eighteen inches tall. Jason was the first to say, "I've never seen that big of a Woodpecker before."

"Look at what a bright red head he has."

"He must be new to Merrysville. I hope he stays here." Everyone nodded.

Amanda told Joyce and the boys to be sure and make a list to tell their parents about all the different birds they saw on their way to the barn. Joyce smiled at her friends and said, "This has been a fun morning already, despite this chilly fog. I think we've seen every kind of bird there is around here." Joyce wasn't going to let fog dampen her joyful spirit.

As soon as she had spoken, nine Geese, flying low in a formation pattern, scared the kids with the loudest honking noises they had ever heard. The Geese were landing in the pond around the corner. Jason laughed and said, "Well, add Geese to your lists." Jimmy laughed but asked, "What?" Jason shrugged his shoulders and said, "Geese are birds. Aren't they?"

Chapter Six

Gaining the Courage
to Enter the Barn

"Cock-a-doodle-doo! Cock-a-doodle-doo!" The children were less than a block from the entrance to their favorite park when the crowing began again. The children turned off the main park road at the sign showing an arrow and a large barn. As they were approaching the old, weathered barn, their laughter and speed seemed to slow down as the crowing grew louder and harsher.

The two girls rubbed their arms, hoping the goosebumps would go away. Every child walking toward that ever-increasing threat tried to ignore the roosters' piercing eyes that continued to look directly at them. This was the first time the children had seen how vicious the roosters looked that close. Amanda's stomach was making a funny noise. She felt a little scared and turned around to look at the boys.

"Cock-a-doodle-doo! Cock-a-doodle-doo!" How could any small animal make such a threatening noise? Each kid thought every rooster was looking directly at him or her. Amanda looked toward Joyce and said, "I can't stand those piercing eyes! Those talons could tear a bear apart! Why did we agree to go inside that barn today?"

Amanda was not a ten-year old coward, but she was being honest with her best friend. Joyce felt the same way but needed to reassure herself and Amanda that it was going to be fun. She laughed and wrinkled her nose before she said, "It's going to be great Amanda! I can just feel it." Her stomach gurgled, and she wasn't feeling nearly as brave as she tried to sound. Amanda was nearly trembling when she saw Joyce wrinkle her nose.

Joyce and Amanda had reluctantly agreed to join Bob, Jimmy, and their friends on this early morning excursion. That was yesterday afternoon when they were safe, playing hopscotch on their friend Abby's sidewalk. Exploring a haunted barn seemed like a scary but fun adventure. Not so, this early on a foggy morning.

The barn was huge; as they walked closer, the barn appeared to loom toward them in the thick fog. Since it had never been painted, it looked old, abandoned, haunted, and very eerie.

On most Friday mornings, the children would have been on their way to school, but yesterday was the last day of school until September. They wanted to do something new and different in the summer of 1946. After all, they were going into the sixth grade in September. World War II had been over for a year and the world felt like a different place to everyone this year. In a little more than two weeks, many children from the village would begin working several hours a week in the gardens and orchards for Mr. Martin. For the next ten days, the kids were going to take advantage of their freedom.

Often, in the past, when they were within four hundred feet of the old building, one of the kids would point out how weather-beaten the barn was and wondered if it was even safe to get near it. The kids sometimes felt sure that they heard creepy, creaking, moaning noises blaring out of that barn. Joyce whispered to Amanda, "I think that the boys' imaginations have convinced them that the noises made in the barn aren't made by the wind, nor the chick.., oops I mean roosters. Sometimes I feel the same way."

Amanda's voice was shaky as she looked at Joyce and said, "I can't believe it is inhabited by anything except ghosts and their evil roosters. Most of the other barns in the area have open windows on all side walls. Other than the big window where the roosters stand, it looks like all other windows and doors on the front and sides of this barn are always closed. Is it my imagination or do you think the doors and windows could be permanently nailed shut?"

That possibility made both girls shudder and swallow hard. A nagging concern made Amanda turn around and question, "Boys, if we get inside that barn, what if somehow, we can never get out?" Joyce and all the boys looked toward the barn.

There were tall bushes and trees all around the outside walls. Many of the bushes had purple, pink or white flowers on them, which made the barn seem darker. No one seemed to notice the wonderful scent they provided. The shadows from the early morning sun, trying to clear the damp fog, added to the mysterious possibilities.

Trying to sound brave, Bob answered, "Don't worry about it. Maybe we won't even be able to get in. Since none of us has ever walked around to the back of the barn, we don't know for sure that the barn even has a back entrance, or even a back wall. It's possible that the back was ripped off by that tornado eight years ago, which we hear so much about. Maybe there is a 'No Trespassing' sign on the building."

A look of fear passed through the group of children. They looked to their left. There appeared to be a driveway that went around to the back of the barn. None of the children knew where the driveway ended, since no one had ever ventured to follow the driveway, nor was brave enough to get to know anything more about it.

Chapter Seven

Railroad Tracks

The large barn was across a fence from railroad tracks. Just then, a long freight train blew its whistle, followed by a large, grey puff of smoke that filled the air around the barn. The smoke seemed to be loaded with thick black soot and smelled strange. As the train passed behind the barn, the large black engine suddenly appeared in the space behind the driveway. The train engineer spotted the kids, waved, and yelled a greeting from his high workstation. The kids all smiled and waved their hands in a return greeting.

It seemed to calm their fears for a minute, and Jimmy suggested that they count the different cars. Each one concentrated on making his or her count accurate. When the caboose finally passed the left side of the barn, the conductor stood on the back steps and waved to the children.

They smiled and waved back at the cheerful man. Jimmy blurted out, "I counted one hundred and twenty-nine cars."

Everyone must have been concentrating on the cars because they all agreed with Jimmy's counting.

The roosters seemed to be scared by the train and had disappeared from the window. The children relaxed and Bob explained, "Several times a day, freight trains pass closely behind the barn. During World War II, trains were an important means of transportation. These tracks were busy with troop trains taking young soldiers, airmen, marines, and sailors from their homes to a military base.

From their base, they were often sent overseas to fight for our country.

Immediately after WWII ended, troop trains passed through town for several months to return the military personnel back to their hometowns. This year, in 1946, it's rare to see even one troop train a week. We can thank God that most of the military men and women are home."

Chris told about all the trains that stop in Merrysville in the fall and winter to pick up grain from the elevators. Every kid spoke up, one at a time, and told something about the trains that go through town. Some felt they were noisy; some liked the fact that they could hear the whistle when it was a mile out of town as it passed White's Crossing near the cemetery. Almost everyone agreed that when they go anywhere in the family car, their dad or mom often must stop the car at the crossings to let the train pass.

Amanda spoke up and made everyone laugh when she said, "It's interesting that most of you like hearing the trains passing White's Crossing. I don't notice it during the day, but at night I cover my head with my sheet when I hear the forlorn sound that the train whistle makes at White's Crossing, and as they get near the crossings in town." Most of the kids said they were often at the ponds fishing when trains stopped at the huge water tower to fill their tank. Jimmy made a face and simply said, "Please!" Everyone laughed.

Chapter Eight

Roosters, Roosters, but who else lives in the barn?

O h no! There it was again! "Cock-a-doodle-doo! Cock-a-doodle-doo!" The roosters had returned and were once again making a horrible racket. Joyce nearly screamed, "Oh no, look! There are more roosters than there usually are!" Every one of the kids had already noticed. One of the boys answered, "We can see them, but where did they come from?" The inside of the barn looked very dark behind the crowd of noisy, bright-colored roosters.

Amanda's stomach was making a funny noise. She really felt scared and turned around to look at the boys.

Other stomachs were churning. As they walked closer to the barn, the boys stopped to whisper to each other. Bob swallowed hard, and then admitted, "Maybe going into a dark barn this early in the morning might not be the best idea for the girls."

Jimmy nodded and then added, "What if we couldn't see the many animals that just might live in that barn?" Another friend added, "What if a raccoon jumps out on us?

Wouldn't the girls be frightened?

I've heard that raccoons bite. Couldn't someone get hurt?" Another boy confirmed that raccoons not only bite but could outrun humans. One of the boys was starting to feel queasy. He held his hand over his mouth, hoping not to throw up in front of his friends.

The short plump boy, Jason Hanaway, looked frightened, when he suddenly whispered, "What if a family of skunks happens to live in the barn?" He had a tear in his eyes as he continued, "They'd probably wet all over us, and our families wouldn't even want us to come into our houses ever again."

All the boys felt fearful and nodded. "What if a bull that hates people lives in that big barn?" Bob spoke quietly when he added, "I don't know if it's true, but I heard that snakes often live under the straw in barns. Have any of you ever heard that? What if the girls are right? What if we couldn't run fast enough to get out of there if we had to?"

All the boys were beginning to think the worst. Some admitted they had heard all kinds of stories about snakes. Jimmy spoke up again, "How could we protect ourselves, as well as the girls, if those roosters attacked us?" Just as they were about to tell the girls that they had changed their minds, and they would explore the barn on another day, later in the day, a truck drove down the driveway toward the barn.

Chapter Nine

Mr. Spitznaugle to the Rescue

Ah! It was Mr. Spitznaugle driving his beautiful new red Ford pickup. The boys exchanged relieved looks and secretly sighed a sigh of relief.

The red truck stopped when the kids who knew him shouted, "Hello Mr. Spitznaugle!" Those kids liked Mr. Spitznaugle. He was a friend of their dads, and an elder and the Sunday School Superintendent at their church. He always took time to talk to the kids at church, and he always had a smile for them.

They knew he liked them. He had held them in his arms when they were carried to the front of the church as babies to be dedicated to the Lord. He planned to start teaching the 6th grade Sunday School class in September.

He was pleased to see that children from the church had their friends with them. As the kids gathered near his truck, Mr. Spitznaugle leaned out of his truck window. "Well, good morning boys and girls. It's good to see all of you are awake and on your way to a fun adventure." He paused, "Have any of you ever gone into my barn?" All the kids were glad that they were able to shake their heads.

"Why no, Mr. Spitznaugle; we knew it was someone's private property," answered Joyce. "My parents told us that it didn't belong to the park." Mr. Spitznaugle smiled as he told the kids, "Why don't you just call me Mr. Andy? That's what your parents call me." All the boys and girls liked that idea and smiled as they yelled their "OK" at the same time.

Mr. Andy jumped out of his truck. In his tan cotton work clothes, he looked taller than his five-foot, nine-inch frame looked at church when he usually was wearing a black suit and grey tie. His tan cotton cap covered most of his thinning brown and grey hair. A big smile was on his clean-shaven, tanned face as he looked into the eyes of each girl and boy.

He looked at Jimmy and asked, "Why Jimmy Martin, what happened to your mouth and lip? Are those stitches holding your upper lip together?" A grin came across Jimmy's face as he nodded and answered Mr. Andy, "Well, it really was my own fault. Bob Perkins and I were running away from some hornets that were chasing us around the park. I was so busy dodging the hornets that I didn't notice the big rock and I tripped over it."

"If I hadn't been wearing these braces, the orthodontist said I would have lost my two front teeth." Jimmy smiled, showing his front teeth, and continued, "Since they're my permanent teeth, he said I would have been up a creek, without a paddle.

The braces saved my teeth but cut my top lip and gum."

"As you can see, my knees and elbows also got badly scraped." Mr. Andy eyed the scrapes, but looked puzzled when he asked Jimmy, "Why are you blaming yourself for the accident, Jimmy? Falling on that rock could have happened to anyone who was trying to outrun hornets."

"Oh, it was my fault all right," Jimmy replied. "My friend Bob told me not to throw that big rock up in the tree and knock down the hornets' nest. If I had listened to him, the hornets would not have been chasing us. Fortunately, when I fell, the hornets flew away."

"Bob lifted me up, blood and all, then we walked home together." Jimmy ended his explanation with a smile and a giggle. Every muscle in Mr. Andy's face became a smile as he raised his arms, and his laugh was almost a roar. Some of the kids were giggling so hard, they were holding their sides. Most of them were like Mr. Andy; they had to wipe the laughter tears from their cheeks as they looked at Jimmy and smiled.

Bob looked serious as he nodded, then quickly said, "He was bleeding all over the place." Bob was kind and did not mention that Jimmy had also been crying hard. Bob continued, "When we got to his house, after Mrs. Martin cleaned him up, she had me ride with her and Jimmy to the Emergency Room, then to the dentist." Jimmy corrected him, "It was my orthodontist." Bob nodded.

Mr. Andy patted Jimmy on the shoulder and told everyone, "Jimmy has a lot to be thankful for. First, that God had those hornets go away; second, that he was with his friend Bob, and third, that he didn't lose those front teeth." Many of the children smiled and said, "Amen."

Jimmy was still smiling when he shared the lesson that the incident had taught him. "I learned to think before I act and not to yield to a temptation that could damage anything. Oh yeah, and to listen to wise advice. Ignoring it certainly had its consequences."

Jimmy introduced his other friends to Mr. Andy. Jimmy put his arms around the two boys, and enthusiastically announced, "Jason and Chris are coming to church with us this Sunday."

"They've never gone to Sunday School before." The girls were pleasantly surprised. Joyce looked at the boys and said, "Oh-h-h! Way to go! That's great, boys." Everyone smiled and nodded.

Mr. Andy was thinking, "These boys and girls will be in my Sunday School class when I start teaching sixth graders this fall."

Chapter Ten

The History of the Barn

A big smile was on his face and pride in his voice as Mr. Andy told them the history of the barn. The kids knew that it was the most talked-about barn in the county. "A little more than eighty years ago, my grandpa and dad inherited over two thousand acres of land in this area. At that time there was no village here, just a large farm. The farm had land, barns, sixteen horses, and five houses when they arrived."

"The large white house where I now live, belonged to Grandpa and Grandma Spitznaugle; the four-bedroom tan house behind the big house belonged to Dad and Mom; and the three smaller three-bedroom houses that are a block from our house were used by the hired hands and their families. My farm managers still live in two of those houses. A hired hand on the farm lives in the third house."

A friend of Bob's spoke up, "I know his son. That's a nice house."

Mr. Andy smiled and continued, "Thank you. Three hired hands who were bachelors, lived in our four-bedroom house for several years."

"One died and the other two retired just before Grandpa and his family arrived to claim their inheritance." Every young face was watching Mr. Andy and each was listening intently.

Mr. Andy moved his right hand in a broad circle to point out the area where they stood. He continued, "Right away my family discovered that more than fifty-six acres contained two sunken holes and what looked like a mountain of gravel. The fifty-six acres were mostly gravel, and unsuitable for farming. Many trees surrounded the gravel area on the spot where we are standing. Several of these trees were here then." The children looked at the trees and wondered how old those trees must be now.

"Shortly after their arrival, Dad married my mother, and I was born in 1888. They missed living in Ft. Wayne, Indiana, the largest city north of our farm. My mother and grandma missed having neighbors. So did Dad and Grandpa. One big question was, 'What should they do with fifty-six acres of gravel and trees, acres of woods and pastureland, plus more than a thousand acres of farmland?'"

"After all, three workers were gone; they only had three hired hands and eight teams of horses to work on the farm." Jason was jumping up and down, with his hand in the air, "I think they would just give away the gravel. Did they?" Jimmy looked at Jason and asked, "Why would they do that?"

Mr. Andy laughed and answered, "Good guess, but no, they didn't. After Dad and Grandpa tried helping the three men at farming many of the remaining acres for one year, they decided that they didn't enjoy being farmers."

"The three hired hands were professional farmers and advised Dad and Grandpa that neither of them belonged on a workhorse or behind a plow. He reminded them that in the past, their family farmed a few hundred acres one year, then rotated each year. They let many acres serve as pastures for the horses and cattle they used to raise."

"The three hired hands reminded them that it would be impossible for the three of them to farm the acreage, not used for pastures. If most of the land was to be farmed, my family had some choices to make.- One, they could hire at least three additional experienced hired hands, buy more teams of horses and make a plan of rotation; Two, they could rent out many acres to farmers and let the three of them farm what they could; or Three, they could sell parcels of land for houses, farm part of the land, do something with the acres of gravel, and keep the hundreds of acres of beautiful woods. My family should make a long-range plan and decide just what you they hoped to do with it."

"Grandpa and Dad agreed with them. The two of them met with their employees and discussed which acres would be the best six hundred acres of farmland to continue farming.

They hired two more employees to help on the farm and agreed to make a plan of what to do with the remaining land."

Bob was curious, "Mr. Andy, where is that large mountain of gravel that you mentioned?" Mr. Andy answered, "Good question Bob. It was a huge pile of good gravel right where the big fishing pond is."

"After my family looked at it and gave it much thought, they decided to build a factory."

"They decided to use their gravel to make nice bricks. Bricks have been used for sidewalks, city streets, patios, and buildings, including houses, for many years. They hired several men to construct a building large enough to use as a factory, with an office area. The large brick-lined furnace, which needed to serve as a kiln to dry the bricks, was located at the back of the building with lots of windows and ventilation. The large office at the front of the brick factory housed several employees who were needed to run their many businesses. The gravel was excellent quality and there was a lot of it."

"They also decided to sell it to contractors to make cement blocks and to build cement basement walls. Most of the neighboring towns built their streets with our bricks. You walk on many of those bricks every time you walk on the sidewalks or cross the streets of Merrysville. Most of the paths in the park used our original bricks. Your parents could tell you about many streets and sidewalks where our bricks are still being used in other towns and cities."

Jimmy turned and looked toward the short cement block wall on their left. The children had made guesses about that wall during the many times they had passed this way. Jimmy asked, "Excuse me for interrupting you Mr. Andy, but why did our village build such a big cement fence around the picnic area and the huge play area instead of just around the picnic tables?"

Mr. Andy pointed toward the antique sign on the corner post of the large, well-groomed picnic area on his left. A neat short cement wall appeared to surround nearly a city-block square of neatly mowed grass. He looked serious as he explained, "Jimmy, that wall was the outside frame for the factory where the bricks were made. When the factory building was up and running, my family began a construction company to build houses and business buildings. One business led to another."

"Wow!" It was all that Jimmy could say, but all the kids seemed to be spellbound.

Mr. Andy continued, "The five farmhands, using workhorses, couldn't possibly work the entire fourteen hundred and forty acres of farmland. They could continue farming the six hundred acres. Dad and Grandpa sold two farms of two hundred fifty acres each. They rented out the remaining farmland to three farmers. I still own this farmland and our original 600-acre farm."

"Dad and Grandpa decided to divide the acreage nearer to the gravel pits, into one-half acre, one-acre and two-acre lots. Employees and people from neighboring cities and towns bought the lots, had houses or stores built, and the village of Merrysville was born."

Joyce interrupted, "Who built the buildings? Was our house one of them, Mr. Andy?" Mr. Andy shook his head and continued, "No, not at that time, it wasn't. After the factory was completed, the men who built the factory were employed to make bricks there, work for the family construction company, work on the farm, or to help around the gravel pits. There were many jobs."

"The businesses were quickly becoming successful for the employees and my family. Their bricks were considered of excellent quality, and my family got rich." Amanda put her fingers to her lips, let out a loud whistle, and shouted, "Wow-e-e! That's some success story." Everyone laughed.

Joyce interrupted, "Going back to that wall, none of us can understand the sign, 'Dedicated to' ...and then twenty names are listed. Who were those twenty men?"

Mr. Andy continued, "After the factory had been there for more than twenty years, two acrobatic airplanes collided and crashed into the factory, killing many of the employees. Merrysville did not have a fire department at that time. By the time volunteer firemen and a fire truck arrived from the nearest town, five miles away, the factory had burned down to the cement blocks."

"Neither airplane was insured. After my family had paid for all the employee funerals, and taken care of the surviving families, our family's fortune had dwindled. The construction business and gravel sales kept the remaining employees busy. My family kept the factory site to sell in case of an emergency."

"The town mowed the grass and weeds when they were mowing the park grass. Our family allowed the people to use the tennis courts, picnic tables and playground equipment. Ten years ago, I gave the property to the village on the condition that it would always remain a part of the park. The village can add anything recreational they desire now."

"Joyce, to answer your question, the first eighteen names on the plaque are the names of our employees who died in the fire from the plane crash." He paused as he wiped a tear that fell from his left eye. He looked down, and nearly cried as he added, "All those men were friends of our family. The last two are the names of the pilots."

All the kids were quiet for a moment, and then one by one, they went over and gave Mr. Andy a big hug. He and all the kids wiped the tears from their eyes. Amanda thanked Mr. Andy for all his gifts to the village. Everyone else echoed Amanda's thanks.

Chapter Eleven

Elevators are Important
to Merrysville

On the other side of the tracks were two grain elevators. A street down the middle of the village divided the property of the two huge elevators.

The grain elevators were an important part of Merrysville. Other than Mr. Andy's many businesses, the elevators were the largest employers, and they were the reason that the train went through the village.

Mr. Andy told the children, "The farmers bring their corn, wheat, and other crops to the elevators to be dried and sold. Much of the product is loaded into train cars and transported to companies who make it into flour, cereal, and other food products."

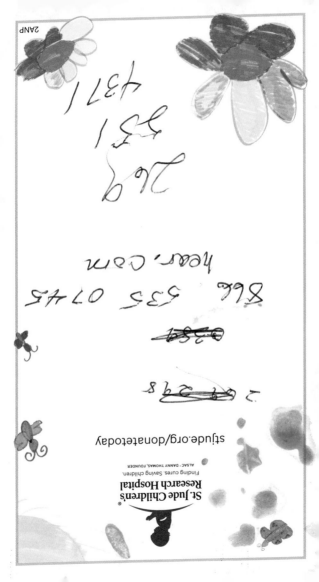

St. Jude Children's Research Hospital

Finding cures. Saving children.
ALSAC · DANNY THOMAS, FOUNDER

stjude.org/donatetoday

866 535 0145
hear.com

"The Family Co-op Elevator, located across the street, is owned by nearly a hundred farmers who bring their harvest there to be processed. The farmers of several small and large farms are local or located in this county."

"The Farmers Local Elevator, located just across the railroad tracks from this barn, is owned by three other businessmen and me." Mr. Andy pointed toward the towering elevator behind his barn. He informed the children, "Corn is dried in the large dryers at the top of the building, and then removed from the cobs."

Jimmy spoke up and said, "Mr. Andy, our dad told us that all farmers are grateful that your family donated the land and had both elevators built. Is that true?" Mr. Andy smiled, nodded, and said, "My parents felt it was an investment in Merrysville." Several kids said something nice about his family's generosity.

Mr. Andy smiled and said, "Thank you." His hand pointed behind the elevator and he continued, "The corncobs are stored in that huge building that you see away from all other elevator buildings. Years ago, that building burned down to the ground because someone sleeping there threw a lit cigarette butt onto the floor. The man died in the fire." All the kids gasped at that news. Jimmy nearly whispered, "Oh my goodness."

"Spitznaugle Farms is one of the biggest users of the public grain elevator. The other three men are the management team for our elevator. Our customers come from farms many miles from here."

"Between World War I and World War II, men looking for work got off the train and slept in that new corncob building. At that time, and even now, local people who don't burn oil are encouraged to go there with burlap cloth bags and take the corncobs home to start fires in their coal stoves for heating their homes on the cold mornings. Most people in town have visited the corncob building."

All the children began talking at once, telling Mr. Andy that they had been there to gather corncobs for their parents. Mr. Andy learned that when one kid was getting ready to go to the corncrib bin, he would call his friends and they made a fun time out of the trip. Mr. Andy was pleased to hear this.

Mr. Andy continued, "Oil was not available for stoves or furnaces of new homes built during the World Wars, and in 1946, there is still no natural gas available in Merrysville for heating homes or cooking. I'm sure you've noticed propane tanks behind many houses." All the kids nodded.

"Everyone in the village knew that strangers from the trains had been seen coming out of that corncob building early in the mornings. It was the only place in town for strangers, with no family here, to sleep. That problem made me feel sorry for the strangers, so I decided to allow people to sleep in my barn. Hardly a week goes by when one or two men do not get off the train and spend at least a night or two here. In fact, one very nice man was here for a while until he got a temporary job working for Amanda and Jimmy's parents."

Jimmy's hand quickly shot up, and before Mr. Andy could acknowledge it, Jimmy blurted out, "Do you mean to tell us that you built this big barn just so people coming off the train had a safe, warm place to sleep?"

Mr. Andy smiled and shook his head. "No," he explained, "The barn was built to provide an office after the building for making bricks burned. We also needed a place for housing the trucks and equipment, and to house the horses in the wintertime. The horse barns on the farm sites are not well insulated and are closed for the winter."

"Dad and I needed a heated place for the employees to meet and pick up the trucks before they went to the building sites. You will see the office and stalls for the horses when I show you the barn. My dad and I were so busy with our other businesses that the barn was never painted."

"The barn is still very sturdy and safe, but ever since Dad died, the entire business has been my responsibility. Neither of my two children are interested in the family businesses, and, after finishing college, both moved to other parts of the country. My wife died, and I have really been busy. I've never taken the time nor money to have the barn painted."

"As most of you know, I now use part of my large office building downtown for my businesses. In the winter, the horses still live in this barn. This winter, you children can come visit them if you would like. If I'm here, you could even ride them around the inside of the barn. I'm sure they'd appreciate that." All the kids smiled and agreed with Bob's, "Wow! That sounds like fun." The kids' eyes were as big as saucers as they all let Mr. Andy know that they would plan on it.

Chapter Twelve

Who Invented the Ponds?

Amanda asked Mr. Andy, "Can you tell us where the ponds came from? Did you dig the ponds, and did the fish just appear?" Mr. Andy's head went back as he laughed aloud. He pointed to the three ponds. "The large area, where the gravel hill looked like a mountain, was used first. The mountain quickly disappeared as we went wider and deeper, and we were able to get gravel out of that hole for years."

"As we went deeper and wider, the gravel became too loose for driving trucks safely down into the pit for loading. To make loading the trucks possible, we went to an elevator system that used large conveyor belts to haul the gravel to the surface."

"When the elevators and conveyor belts were down nearly one hundred feet, we discovered that pit number one had a natural spring at the bottom of the huge, deep gravel pit.

Immediately, the water began to fill the pit. It was necessary for the equipment to be quickly removed and brought up to the surface."

"Within two years, the original pit had filled with water. Our family put up warning signs and a fence to prevent anyone from falling into the deep pit. The equipment necessary for loading gravel was moved into pit number two. This allowed gravel from the middle pit to be sold. It was also the excellent grade of gravel that we had been selling out of the first pit."

"To answer your question, Amanda, it was around that time when six truckloads of fish were on their way from Canada to Kentucky to fill a fishery."

"When the fishery had leakage problems, the Kentucky fishery called the company in Canada to postpone the order until their fishery was repaired. Unfortunately, the fish had already been sent."

"The six trucks were gassing up at that Standard gas station, only a few blocks from the gravel pits, when the truck drivers were called on their Citizen Band radios (CB's). The drivers were told to find a place where they could get rid of the fish, and then return to Canada. It just so happened that my dad had stopped at the same gas station." Mr. Andy paused for just a moment, making sure he told the story like he had heard it a hundred times from his dad.

"When Dad heard of their plight, he explained that he owned a large pond, created from a hundred feet deep gravel pit, and offered to let the Canadians dump the fish there. The men didn't charge him anything for the fish, and they were relieved to get rid of their cargo. Talk about luck." A big "Wow!" was heard among the boys.

Joyce's voice boomed. "What a blessing for them and for Merrysville! It's like God knew you boys would love fishing." Everyone agreed.

Mr. Andy continued, "After the truck drivers unloaded the fish and ate the nice meal that my mother cooked for them, they returned to Canada. Because the pit was so large and deep, the fish quickly grew."

Bob was amazed at the explanation, and asked Mr. Andy, "Why did all of the snapping turtles come to this park? My friends and I have never seen them by any of the creeks or rivers around Merrysville."

Mr. Andy laughed and confirmed, "I know that the huge snapping turtles are not native to this part of Indiana. I can't explain where they came from, but I've always suspected that they must have come with the fish."

"I believe the type of snapping turtles that are in and around the park ponds are native to Canada. Unfortunately, when I first wondered about that myself, I was never able to locate the fishery that donated these fish to Dad. I have checked with the Canadian Department of Wildlife. It is also their opinion that these turtles are identical to those in the area where our fish probably were raised."

"Years later, when gravel from pit number two was emptied, pit number three was opened. We are now using gravel from several acres of ours, located about two blocks from the river. We quit selling gravel when these three pits were closed."

Amanda licked her lips, and her expressive eyes were on Mr. Andy as she declared, "Mr. Andy, we're mesmerized just hearing all the details about this area where we love to play." Mr. Andy and the kids all laughed at her declaration.

Mr. Andy looked at Amanda with a smile on his face and replied, "Amanda Martin, your knowledge of big words is amazing. I .."

Jimmy interrupted, "That's true, but the boys and I are excited about getting to see what's inside that big barn. Amanda's such a fraidy cat that she probably won't even go in."

Amanda frowned at her brother and quietly said, "I was afraid when I thought that you boys might not be able to protect yourselves, as well as Joyce and me, but I am sure Mr. Andy can protect all of us."

Mr. Andy turned his head toward Jimmy, and then back to Amanda, "We'll go inside in just a minute Jimmy."

By this time, Jimmy was getting frustrated. He thought Mr. Andy would never stop talking. When Jimmy started to huff and puff, the other kids glared at him. He couldn't believe it! He was disappointed that his friends wanted to hear more.

Amanda smiled and asked, "Can you tell us how that tree that is growing on its side and lying partway across the middle pond, ever got there, and what prevents it from just falling into the water?"

"Good question Amanda. That tree was growing straight up for several years, then during a tornado - or bad windstorm - people called it different things – the tree was nearly uprooted, but many of the strong roots have held it there. It has been there for about twenty years, and as you can see, it keeps getting taller. The top branches are almost reaching the land on the other side of the water. Some of its large limbs must be underwater holding it in place."

As soon as Amanda asked the question, her mind drifted to the many times she had secretly walked down the trunk of that fallen tree in the summer and relaxed on the comfortable branches that were hidden by the leaves. She often went there to meditate and write her poetry. Her thoughts remembered yesterday.

"My private tree – a desk lying on its side,

As I write poetry on the trunk, so wide.

Branches serve as my chair,

Turtles join me – seems they're everywhere,"

Ever since she got to know the many snapping turtles that used the tree for their sunning, they became friends, and recognized the names Amanda had given them. Joyce nudged Amanda when she realized that she was daydreaming. Amanda smiled to let Joyce know she was back to reality.

Mr. Andy continued, "When the fish were growing quickly in pit one, many people living in the area asked if they could fish in the gravel pit. Thirty years ago, my family agreed to charge five dollars for an annual family membership."

"State fishing laws were required to be obeyed by all family members to fish whenever they chose. My family had our builders slope the edges of the pit, gradually for sixty or seventy feet all around, to make them safe. As you know, we have signs posted telling everyone that the pond is one hundred feet deep. That is why the strong fences will always surround the drop-off of that pond."

Mr. Andy was still sitting on the back of his truck, resting his chin on his right knee, when he continued, "I donated all of my land occupied by the ponds to the village of Merrysville to be used as a park."

"Only residents of the township are invited to be members of the fishing club. Merrysville continues to charge five dollars a year for a family membership."

"This village is small, but most large cities don't have a 'fishing hole'."

"I'm glad you use it." Every kid was thinking, "Me, too."

Mr. Andy noticed the boys were anxious to get into the barn, but continued, "The employees did some landscaping, and I bought the sturdy red park benches for sitting around the ponds. My employees keep them in good repair and paint them every spring."

"After the gravel in ponds number two and three was removed down to the natural springs, they soon filled with water. My dad and I had the ponds, one at a time, connected by having forty feet wide and ten feet deep channels dug between the ponds, making the long chain of ponds."

As if it was an afterthought, Mr. Andy nearly whispered, "I'm sure that normal erosion has caused the depth between the ponds to be even greater than ten feet." As the girls were smiling and nodding their heads, he continued, "My family was officially out of the gravel business."

"I added the sturdy fifty feet walking bridges over each channel, with benches for the members of the fishing club. Although many of the fish swim in all the ponds, I'd be safe to say that the bottom of the large pond still holds most of the largest fish."

"When I became a father, I added the swings and playground equipment near the tennis courts in the recreation square. Many couples play on the courts while their children are entertained by the playground. The village built the Square Dance building near the tennis courts. People come from miles around to dance in that building."

"A village Councilman volunteered to build a large sign to identify our park. 'Welcome to Merrysville Park, Home of the Three Ponds' has been used for thirty years. Thus, they became known as the Merrysville Ponds."

Chapter Thirteen

We Need history

Mr. Andy answered every question that the children asked him. The boys were fidgeting as they continually thought of getting in and out of the barn, so they could go fishing before the sun got any hotter.

Bob told Mr. Andy, "I'm amazed to learn the history of the beautiful village park. I really do not believe that most of the residents of Merrysville know much about our village history. I know our parents would have told us if they knew."

"Could you ask everybody on Decoration Day at the dedication of the village signs, how many know this story? If most don't, would you tell them some of these things?"

Jimmy was thinking that he wished the kids would stop asking questions. As he glanced at his watch, he added, "We'd love to hear about everything then." Joyce spoke up, "Have you considered maybe writing a brochure about it before

Decoration Day? The print shop could print it, and everyone could have a copy at the unveiling of the sign."

Her voice became very dramatic as she added, "I'm sure it would be a keepsake; I'd keep it forever." Everyone declared it would be one of his or her favorite keepsakes. They had no idea of the cost of such a project. Mr. Andy promised to consider it.

"Now that you've learned all about the park, let's go inside so you can see the barn." A sigh of relief came from every boy there. "I come to this barn early every morning to feed my chickens, roosters, and cats, and to collect the eggs. Our local grocery store has fresh eggs every day for your families. Probably none of you, or your friends, ever gave it a thought, but if you did, no wild animals live in the barn." Every kid was relieved to hear that revelation.

"Now, why don't you kids come into the barn to meet my animals?" They all nodded and were happy to finally have the opportunity.

The boys put their fishing poles and rods in the back of the red truck and followed behind. Bob turned around to Jimmy and whispered, "Finally!"

It was evident that all the boys were getting bored. The fog was gone and the sun brightly shining. Quite some time had passed since Mr. Andy had driven into the barnyard driveway. The boys liked Mr. Andy, but they now realized that he was like the girls, he enjoyed talking too much.

As they walked on the path, toward the barn, they stopped in their tracks when they were greeted with yet another, "Cock-a-Doodle-Doo!! Cock-a-Doodle-Doo!!" The shrill greeting from the ferocious looking roosters resumed and resonated throughout the lovely village park, even alarming the ducks that were asleep on their nests near the barn. Many of the ducks stood, shook their wings, turned around, looked at the eggs they were sitting on, and returned their warmth to their nests.

The crowing must have awakened all the roosters in the barn. After what seemed like only a few seconds, the large haymow window was loaded with many more roosters, each wearing the thick multi-colored feathers of beautiful dark shades of red, orange, green, and yellow. The crowing reverberated like an angry orchestra.

As they walked closer to the barn, the trees and bushes surrounding the three ponds seemed to have absorbed much of the sharpness of the sound of the crowing. It did not, however, lessen the fear being felt by the children. Not one word was even whispered, and there was no hero, no bravery displayed.

Proud roosters standing guard in the upper window appeared to be deciding whether, or not, to jump on these unwanted intruders if they came any closer to their domain. The children fearfully followed the path leading to Mr. Andy's truck. No one knew if it would be safe to run.

With each step that passed closer to the barn, the louder the warning sounds blared. The eyes in the barn must have had a glow of fierce red as the intruders continued toward their domain; actually, that was what all the children feared they would see if they had the courage to look directly at the roosters.

When Mr. Andy noticed, he stopped the red truck, got out, and came around to the front of the barn. "Hold it!" Mr.

Andy yelled as he raised his right hand. "Do you want my friends to call all of you, 'The Birds that Bellowed'?"

His eyes danced as he laughed, shook his head, and looked at the noisy chorus of roosters. Again, he reminded the multi-colored orchestra to mind their manners, that these visitors were friends of his.

The piercing eyes of the beautiful birds still stared into the kids' eyes, but the shrillness was reduced to a calm greeting.

As Mr. Andy quickly went around the paved walkway, the children were right behind.

Mr. Andy got back into his truck to drive it around to the back of the huge barn. As the kids arrived, Mr. Andy was already getting animal feed and milk out of the truck. The boys ran to help him carry it inside. A sign on a large door greeted the kids, "Welcome to the Barn that Crows!"

Chapter Fourteen

The Barn that Crows

Seeing the appropriate sign caused all the children to smile. There were three doors in the back of the barn. One large sliding door was there for trucks to drive equipment, horses, hay, straw, and other supplies into the barn; it was locked. The door on the left had a sign telling people they were welcome to stay the night and gave them a list of rules to follow. The third one did not have any hardware on it and appeared not to be used anymore. The girls nodded to each other; both thought it was locked on the inside.

The kids were surprised when Mr. Andy turned on several light switches as they entered the big barn that they had passed so many times on their adventures. There were four or five bright overhead lights that let them see the entire first floor of the huge barn. Amanda suspected the light switches also controlled lights on the upstairs ceiling.

Everyone noticed there were no strange noises inside. Every one of the children was amazed at the vast space inside the barn. They were not expecting to see everything so clean, and all contents well organized.

Mr. Andy pointed out where his office had been, with the built-in desk and bookshelves still standing in their original space. He reminded them that his 2-floor office building is now in the center of the village, next to the drugstore; the eight-stall building behind his downtown office holds the trucks for his builders, and his large construction equipment is housed on the farm outside of town.

Remembering their conversation earlier, Joyce motioned for Amanda to notice the two doors in the office area that had padlocks on them. It was obvious that one of them was the door outside that wasn't used. The girls smiled and once more nodded. The sign on the other door identified it as, "To Pump/ Well Room." There was also a small restroom right outside of the office area. Next to it was a furnace. A barn with a furnace surprised everyone. On the right side of the doors going outside was a large sink. Amanda figured it was for the hired hands to clean their hands, as well as feeding water to the many animals who claimed this barn as home.

Near the office were six neat double stalls for the horses to occupy in the wintertime. Two of them were filled with neatly stacked hay. One of the boys looked at the stalls and asked, "Mr. Andy, now that the war is over and you can get gas for your tractors, what will you do with your horses?"

Mr. Andy explained, "Farmers were able to buy fuel for their tractors during World War II if they were growing food, so we only have four horses now."

"They are currently in pasture and housed in the barns on the farms where they once plowed the land during the spring, summer, and autumn seasons. These horses are getting old; I have had them for many years.

My family has had to bury several horses." He looked serious, and then Mr. Andy said, very simply, "We love those horses that have served us so well, so we'll feed them and house them as long as they live."

"If they aren't well, we have a vet come and take care of them." None of the children said anything but they all noticed the single tear that fell from Mr. Andy's right eye.

As Joyce looked around, she finally relaxed. She was sure that Mr. Andy could protect them if there was any danger. Like Amanda, she was surprised outside when so many additional roosters appeared out of hiding with the original guardian roosters. Amanda wondered if there were more, somewhere upstairs, just waiting. Could Mr. Andy protect them if all the roosters decided to attack them at one time?

The barn had many bales of straw on three sides of the huge first floor room. The straw was stacked all the way to the ceiling.

Mr. Andy explained, "Bales of straw make wonderful insulation to help keep my animals and visitors warm in the winter months. It also keeps the barn cooler in the summer."

As soon as they entered, many cats and several young kittens seemed to come out of the bales of straw. Each feline wanted Mr. Andy and the kids to pet them as they purred. The kids leaped at the opportunity to do so. There were many different colors and breeds of cats and kittens. Mr. Andy was proud to announce, "These cats are great mousers. We never have any mice, rats, or unwanted animals in this barn. Of course, we never have any open food or scraps here."

"That helps."

The kids were surprised to see several folded cots along one section of the straw. On a shelf near the cots, several warm blankets were stacked. Above the cots was a metal sign with several rules on it.

Mr. Andy explained, "There are still many people in the United States who do not have work because recovery from the Great Depression is still felt in 1946."

"Also, WWII was finally over just last year, and many jobs were returned to the veterans who held the jobs before they were drafted to fight in the war. This resulted in many Americans being displaced from their jobs. Those people often relocate to find decent-paying positions."

"Other than looking in the newspaper or knowing someone with a job opening, some feel forced to leave home and go to other states in search of the available jobs."

"Many people are without money to run their cars, if they even have one, forcing them to hitchhike on the roads. Some of the people choose to ride in the boxcars of the trains that pass one hundred yards away from the barnyard and park grounds. Although it is illegal as far as the railroads are concerned, hiding and riding in an empty boxcar cost nothing."

"People illegally riding the boxcars don't enjoy breaking the law; they just have no money for train fare. Many men jump from the boxcars when the train gets near a city or village and slows down, to see if they are lucky enough to find work there."

"Their families plan to join the men in the city or village once they have found a job."

Although the kids were young, their expression of concern pleased Mr. Andy. He knew that he was going to enjoy that sixth grade class at church.

"To prevent the men from having to sleep on the straw or cold floor, I bought the cots so anyone getting off the train here could sleep on a cot, inside the sheltered barn. Some people in America refer to the men as bums, hobos, or tramps."

"This village chose to call them transients."

"I do need to warn you children that most of these men might be Christians and honest people, but there is the possibility that some of them might be fleeing from the law for crimes that they have committed."

Mr. Andy asked how many of them had met Frank Johnson, the nice man who was working for Mr. and Mrs. Martin. Everyone smiled and nodded. Mr. Andy explained, "Frank slept in my barn for several nights until he was hired for the summer to do many jobs for Jimmy and Amanda's parents. He has turned out to be an excellent worker and a Christian who had traveled for nearly two weeks before coming to Merrysville and landing that job."

Jimmy spoke up and told everyone, "He is so nice, and for the moment, he is living in Amanda's playhouse. It is only until he has found a full-time, year-round job in town. Then his family will sell their house and move here." Amanda spoke up and shared, "Our parents hope to increase production this year so they can hire him full time."

Each of the children was able to share a story about a transient who had visited their home, hoping to eat a decent meal in exchange for work.

Mr. Andy urged the children not to talk to strangers without their families being present. "The village has public restrooms and shower rooms behind the fire station. You should never go down that alley. A village employee cleans these rooms and restocks towels, soap, and toilet paper daily. I think this is a kind and caring village." Pride in their village brought tears to most of the children.

As they shared their stories, Mr. Andy poured a gallon of rich cream into several bowls on the floor that were there for that purpose. This cream came from the cows on one of his farms. The cats and kittens quickly shared the treat, and then returned to their hideouts in the bales of straw. One of the boys said, "Where did they go? It's impossible to see any openings in the straw that are big enough for the cats to fit. Does anyone see where they are?" Everyone shook his or her head. Mr. Andy laughed and told the kids that he always wonders the same thing.

Bob asked their kind friend, "Mr. Andy, would you be angry if my friends and I drew a hopscotch board on the cement floor so we could play inside this big building if it was raining outside?" Mr. Andy answered, "Bob, you and your friends have my approval to play inside anytime, if there are no transients here. In the winter, it is warm in here for the transients and animals. I'm pleased that you children would consider this as a playground. I still remember the fun my son and daughter had here."

The kids followed Mr. Andy as he climbed up the wall ladder at the back of the barn. Joyce and Amanda felt uneasy when they thought the roosters would be there waiting for them. Instead, about one hundred hens and small families of chicks greeted them. As Mr. Andy put the chicken feed into the troughs, the chickens ate their breakfast. The large water bottles were filled with fresh water from a sink upstairs that was immediately over the sink on the first floor. Everyone slowly followed Mr. Andy to the front of the building where the roosters lay claim to the second-floor territory.

The feet of these roosters reminded Amanda of the ferocious looking talons on eagles or vultures. They seemed to be pointing at the children as they approached. Joyce and Amanda shuddered. The brave boys felt just as vulnerable, but they put on their brave act. As they neared their territory, the girls whispered to each other regarding the roosters' talons that seemed even more dangerous because of the extra toes on the sides of each foot that they recognized when they were closer to the roosters. Even the boys noticed their extra-long snarly looking toenails and wicked beaks.

To everyone's surprise, the roosters quickly flew up onto the top bales of straw that filled much of the second floor. They appeared to be afraid of the children. They stayed on the straw while Mr. Andy filled their food troughs and water bottles. The roosters then flew down to the floor to consume their food and water. They ignored the kids who stood with their mouths wide-open, staring at the roosters that they had feared for so long.

As they were leaving the haymow, the boys nearly jumped down the stairs behind Mr. Andy. "Finally!" they thought. Their original plan that morning when they left home was to spend a few minutes exploring the barn with the girls, then to go fishing.

"If you follow the path, the area behind the ponds has good mushrooms that your parents find in the spring. I gathered a large bowl full yesterday morning. If you are in the woods with your parents, don't sit down anywhere unless you know it's safe." Mr. Andy instructed the kids about the safe way to check if there is anything under rocks or logs. "Never push a log or rock away from you, but pull it toward yourself, thus allowing bugs, lizards, and snakes to run away from you, instead of up your leg."

"Wow! That's a neat thing to know," said Jimmy. The girls shuddered at the thought, while the boys smiled at the possibility of exploring that area.

Chapter Fifteen

Tennis Anyone?

What a surprise to learn that Mr. Andy had been a scholarship tennis player in college and earned his spending money for college by giving tennis lessons. "When I returned to Merrysville, I gave lessons for years in the evenings after work. Amanda and Jimmy, I believe your parents took lessons from me. My students and I played on the tennis courts right there," he said as he pointed to the courts that were often busy with residents playing tennis. Amanda and Jimmy looked at each other in surprise. Jimmy whispered, "Our parents?"

Mr. Andy nodded and continued, "My dad had it built for that purpose when I was a teenager. I am a tennis instructor at Purdue University, in Lafayette, a city south of here. I also give lessons occasionally here. I'd be happy to teach you kids, free of charge, if you are interested. If you are, just have one of your parents call me to set up a time so that I can reserve the court. After you learn to play, you will need to improve your game by practice."

"When you feel comfortable, I could set up a tournament this autumn between you kids and your parents." All the kids nodded but the boys lacked the enthusiasm that the girls showed about learning the sport. Jason looked a little concerned as he asked, "What if we don't have a tennis racquet?" Mr. Andy laughed and said, "Jason, that is a good question. I have many tennis racquets of different weights. You can use one of them to learn, then maybe your parents will buy you one for your Christmas gift."

The boys quickly excused themselves and told the girls to go swing. The boys retrieved their fishing poles from the back of the shiny red truck and headed toward the big pond to catch some fish.

The girls' minds weren't thinking about sitting on a swing. They could sense that the barn would provide them with the opportunity to make this a special summer if they were allowed to stay inside alone. They were fascinated with all they had learned in one morning.

Amanda told Mr. Andy that she and Joyce didn't know how to play tennis but, in the past, when they thought about learning how to play, all four courts were always full. She asked if kids were allowed to play alone. Mr. Andy explained that there were schedules to sign for the different courts. His face lit up and he suggested, "Look girls, I love to play tennis and to give lessons. Other than Jason, I didn't get the feeling that the boys would be willing to put much effort into learning the game."

"If you two are willing to give up about two hours on Monday, Wednesday, and Friday for lessons, we can schedule one of the courts at a time you are not scheduled to work in the orchards or gardens. If you could practice for an hour after your lessons, I would be happy to schedule your court for three hours."

"I'll teach you all the tricks I taught your parents."

"Knowing how fast you two are at learning anything new, I think it will be fun when you get good enough to challenge your moms to a tournament in seven or eight weeks. If the boys will take lessons and practice, then we could involve your dads too. What do you think?"

The girls found it hard to believe that Mr. Andy would think that highly of them. They both gladly accepted his offer. He suggested that they try to get their parents to buy them a decent tennis racket; having the right weight and size would make a big difference in their games. He explained that tennis rackets were strung with catgut. Of course, neither girl believed his statement, so they laughed. The three agreed to start lessons the following week, in the afternoons, after school.

They discussed many of their thoughts and concerns with Mr. Andy. He told them, "You're welcome to come into the barn anytime it's empty. Before you come into the door, you should look through the side window by the office to make sure that no employees or transients are inside. You just need to promise not to hurt my animals or bring in anything that could cause a fire or leave crumbs. When you play, before you leave, there are several brooms and dustpans to help keep the barn clean."

As they talked, Mr. Andy showed them a secret on the first and second floors. There was an escape route in case they were in the barn and the transients came in. "Behind the straw at the front of the building is another ladder going upstairs. It is not visible to anyone because straw covers it on both floors."

"The second floor has a five-foot wide walking space around the outside wall. It is well hidden by the multiple bales of straw. The front door on the first floor is kept bolted from the inside so no one could come in there. If you ever have an emergency and need to use that door, you must call me immediately when you get home so I can come and keep it locked from the inside. I do not want anyone else to know that that door can be used."

"If you girls have an emergency when you are playing up there and someone is outside near that escape door, there is also a rope ladder that you could use to go down the outside. You would be hidden behind bushes, and you could run around the corner to where my roosters stand guard."

"I installed the rope ladder so, in case of a fire or an emergency, my children or employees could climb down and run along the bushes until they were safely out of the park." Mr. Andy told them about all the fun his children had in that barn when they were young. Wow! That sounded exciting to the girls.

The girls followed Mr. Andy as he climbed the back stairs and showed them the three bales of straw that they would have to move to get inside the walking space. He looked serious when he told the girls, "If you ever do decide you would like to have a secret hiding place upstairs, away from your brothers, be sure to confide in your parents, or at least your moms and me."

"I am sure that your moms would keep your secret. Your parents should know in case they are ever looking for you and can't find you right away. I remember that my children sometimes fell asleep and their mother or I would find them up here." The girls could hardly wait to tell their moms, and to explore it alone sometime.

Amanda looked for Mr. Andy's reaction when she asked him, "Will it hurt the roosters if we bring them a treat sometimes so we can become friends with them?" He smiled as he told them, "That sounds like a good idea." The three went down the stairs toward the back entrance/exit door. Both girls gave him a big smile and thanked him for the tour and invitation to use the barn as a play area whenever they wanted. They promised him that they would always be kind to his animals and never have anything dangerous in the barn.

The three of them went outside. The girls waved to Mr. Andy, walked around the corner, and were running full speed toward the swing set. Both girls had thoughts running through their minds as they swung higher and higher. They both stopped swinging at the same time.

They looked back at the barn and started talking. They began making plans. They wanted to go back into the barn, just the two of them, soon, and see if they could make a hideout in that upstairs space behind the bales of straw. Joyce finally voiced the biggest concern bugging them both, "How do we find a way to make friends with those roosters?"

Chapter Sixteen

A Different Summer

E arly the next morning, Amanda was sitting at the dining room table and talking to her mom about the great meal the night before. She was convinced that her mother was the best cook in the world. Thirty minutes ago, Jimmy went fishing with Bob, Joyce's twin brother. They had fished most of yesterday without a single bite. They thought it was because they started so late in the day when they were learning about the Barn that Crowed.

Joyce pounded on Amanda's front door. Both girls were excited as they told Amanda's mother about all that they and the boys had learned about the park and the animals in the barn. They were careful to let her know that they would depend on her and Joyce's mom to keep their secret.

Joyce was surprised that Amanda or Jimmy had never mentioned anything to their mother last night about the barn.

She and Bob told their parents about everything Mr. Andy had shared with them. Joyce figured that Jimmy probably forgot because he was thinking of that big fish he planned to catch today. She remembered that last night, Bob talked about going fishing today, early.

The boys had not forgotten anything that Mr. Andy had told and shown them. After they left the barn, they were talking about all they had learned while they were supposed to be fishing. All of them were excited about the possibility of hearing more about Merrysville at the sign unveiling in two weeks on Thursday, Decoration Day.

One of the boys even suggested that, if Mr. Andy would be willing to come to school this fall, they might be able to persuade him to share more about the history of the village with all the students.

The girls let Betty know they needed her advice on how to tame those roosters so that they could become friends. Her mom smiled as she suggested, "I think that could be easily solved. Amanda, you may want to take fifty cents out of your piggy bank and go to the grain elevator to buy some special chicken feed."

"The roosters would probably become friends after you girls feed them several times and talk nicely to them." As Amanda's mom talked, the girls looked at each other, smiled and nodded at the simple plan.

Betty Martin agreed that the girls could have the hideout as a secret from the boys if Joyce's mother agreed. Amanda made her mother promise not to tell her brother

Jimmy. Joyce said, "I was so excited just thinking about it that I got my mom's approval this morning before I came over to your house."

"Mom agreed that it should be a secret between you moms and us girls. I must confess that I am very excited about this important opportunity to put some excitement into our lives. I think we're going to hear and do things that we've never experienced before." Amanda was nearly bubbling as she squealed, "Me too!" Amanda's mom felt like she was reliving her past as she witnessed their enthusiasm. She laughed and gave each girl a quick hug.

After she had gotten the money out of her piggy bank, Amanda returned, and told Betty. "Mom, I almost forgot. I would really like to get my own tennis racquet so that Mr. Andy could teach me how to play. Mr. Andy has offered to teach us girls the correct way to play tennis. He isn't going to charge any kids in town who want to learn how to play."

"He surprised Jimmy and me when he told everyone that he had taught you and dad to play." Her mom nodded her head and laughed. Amanda was nearly jumping up and down when she told her mom that when they learned the game, Mr. Andy was going to have the girls play their mothers. Joyce let Betty Martin know that, if the boys took the time to learn to play tennis, Mr. Andy would plan for them to play their dads. Betty thought his plan was great. She smiled as she said, "Somehow I doubt if your dads get to play your brothers." Joyce quickly said, "I think that Mr. Andy thought the same thing." As an afterthought, Betty smiled as she predicted the boys might win their match. "Amanda and Joyce, ask your dads to tell you about some of those games." Betty was nearly snickering as she recalled the frustration that the men sometimes showed when they were defeated so badly.

Betty Martin went into a closet and came back with an old tennis racquet that she handed to Amanda. She said, "I'm so happy to hear that my young daughter is going to take up her parents' favorite game. Mr. Andy and his dad taught us so much about tennis on the court near the barn."

"Before you kids were born, I played tennis every time I had the chance to find someone who was willing to play. In fact, Joyce, your parents and the two of us used to play together once or twice a week. Your mom and I were partners, and usually won."

Betty continued, "In College, your dad and I were members of the school tennis team and often helped win a trophy. I am going to take the time today to go up to the attic and find our trophies. You can see them later, and I'll tell you about each one."

Amanda smiled, "That's neat, Mom. You and Dad are good at everything you do, so I'm not surprised that you won most of the time. I've always been so proud of you."

"Maybe we can play together after I learn how to play. Mr. Andy wants us to take the lessons three days a week, then practice, practice, practice."

Mrs. Martin retrieved the well-worn racquet from Amanda. "For sure I should be using this racquet, so that I can get in some much-needed practice of my own. I will call your mother in a few minutes Joyce. Maybe tomorrow we will take you girls to South Bend to get racquets of your own. It really is important that you choose a racquet that is comfortable in your hand. I might get a new one too."

"Maybe Mr. Andy will be kind enough to give us parents some refresher lessons as well. Did he tell you that he still teaches tennis at Purdue University?" Amanda answered, "Yes he did. Can you tell us what they use to string tennis racquets?" Mrs. Martin laughed and said, "I believe they still string them with catgut. Why do you ask?" Both girls were shocked. Amanda meekly said, "Just curious."

Mrs. Martin placed the tennis racquet carefully on her desk as a reminder.

Amanda told her mother about Mr. Andy's invitation for the kids and their families to visit him in his big house in the afternoons or evenings. Amanda and Joyce learned that their dads and Mr. Andy were good friends and sometimes played checkers and other games together at Mr. Andy's house.

After the girls had discussed more of their hideout plans with Betty, they could see that she was going to be a good help in making those plans work.

Betty put a large, shiny, metal garbage can, with a tight-fitting lid, on the red wagon. In it, she put two empty three-pound syrup cans. She knew the girls could never carry the large can up the stairs if it was full of chicken feed.

She instructed the girls, "As soon as you get to the barn, take this large empty can up to the hideout area first."

"Then you can use the covered three-pound cans to make several trips. Take the chicken feed up to the hideout to store it in the large can."

"To prevent attracting mice or rats, be careful to not drop chicken feed when you are filling the three-pound cans, safely transporting it up the stairs, or later when feeding the roosters. Be sure lids are always on tight. It's very kind of Mr. Andy to give you girls the opportunity to use the barn for a hideout. It sounds like something I would have done at your age if I had the chance. Neither of your brothers or dads would ever guess you would be interested."

After they took the metal cans to their hideout in the barn, Joyce and Amanda followed Betty's advice. The large metal can was heavier than the girls imagined. They took the small cans upstairs first. Amanda was pulling while Joyce pushed the big one up the steps. It took up a lot of room in their hideout. They made room by shifting one bale of straw into another area. They took Amanda's deluxe red Radio wagon to the big grain elevator, across the railroad tracks from the park.

Amanda told the man behind the counter, "We've come to buy fifty cents worth of your best chicken feed." The man laughed and told them, "You'd better have a wheelbarrow. You'll need one to transport a fifty-cent burlap bag of chicken feed." Joyce's deep dimples were showing as she gave the man her sweetest smile and asked, "Would you be strong enough to load it for us?"

The grain salesclerk smiled when he saw the large wagon and told the girls, "Whew! This wagon is even better than a wheelbarrow." The man lifted the heavy burlap bag onto the wagon, and the girls took turns with one pulling and one pushing the heavy load over the railroad tracks, down the park road, and into the barn. The girls made several trips upstairs and through the secret passageway to get the chicken feed stored in the large metal container.

The girls soon learned that Amanda's mom was right about the animals. When the girls came out of their hideout, with their syrup can half-full of the special seed, they walked down to the area where the roosters stood guard. The roosters jumped up onto the straw. As soon as Amanda and Joyce put some of the special feed into the troughs, the chickens and roosters seemed to have lost their fear of the girls and walked bravely past them to enjoy their snack.

When the roosters didn't seem so mean-looking, the girls smiled and softly told the roosters that they were really beautiful. The roosters acted as if they understood what the girls were saying. The girls soon had nicknames for most of the roosters. Whenever the roosters spotted the girls coming alone, they looked forward to their special treats, and their crowing was no longer harsh.

The girls walked around the perimeter of the three walls upstairs to view the area Mr. Andy discussed with them. They moved many bales of straw from behind others and brought them to the front of the stacks. Finally, there was a neat and spacious hideout. It was next to the wall with three bales of straw that served as a blockade to their secret passage.

No one would be able to know the girls were behind the straw. There was a window cranked partway open. They could safely breathe behind the straw and see out, but it was impossible for anyone to see them. From the ground, it looked like straw was the only thing in the barn. They decided that next Tuesday they would bring a canvas cover and a blanket for the hideout. The girls enjoyed knowing that their moms were the only people who knew their new secrets.

Chapter Seventeen

Summer has Begun

The two exhausted girls could hardly climb down the stairs. They knew they had to take a break on the swings before they walked home. Just as Joyce started to say something, three girlfriends came running toward them.

Their friend Abby told the girls, "I can't believe it. Nellie, Phyllis, and I are already bored and school has only been out for two days. Can you girls think of something that will keep us busy after work? Until the day after Decoration Day, we're only working three hours a day, two days a week. We can work six hours a day, four days a week after the holiday when there will be more vegetables to harvest and prepare for market. We're both going to open a savings account at the Savings and Loan. Joyce and Amanda told their friends they had savings accounts there and get interest quarterly that adds to their balance. Both girls encouraged their friends not to use much of the money in their accounts, but to save it toward college.

Amanda was excited to hear that their friends were also going to be working for her dad. She asked them when they found out they got the jobs. All three girls were excited to tell Amanda and Joyce that they had been interviewed by Frank Johnson yesterday and really were looking forward to having him as their boss.

Nellie asked Amanda if it was true that Mr. Johnson was living in her playhouse. Amanda told them how he started working for the Martin Gardens. While the two girls sat on the swings, Joyce turned her swing around and said, "I was so glad that Mr. Andy mentioned Frank Johnson on Friday.

"As Mr. Andy told us, following the Great Depression, and World War 2, most Americans were considerate of people who were unemployed after the war. Most Americans knew someone who was looking for a job."

"Frank Johnson told our family that most Americans think that all servicemen came back from the war and got their old job back. By the time he was discharged from the Navy, the war was over. The company he worked for before he joined the Navy, lost their Defense Supply contract and went out of business."

"Mr. Johnson named the city in Ohio where his family was living. When there were no other jobs in his town, he and many unemployed men and veterans had to leave their homes to look for work in other cities and states. He said his wife and kids would move when he found a permanent job. When he left home, he had no money for rooms nor food.

Amanda told them, "Let me tell you about Frank Johnson and how he started working for the Martin Gardens." While the two girls sat on the swings, Joyce turned her swing around and said, "I'm happy my parents raise vegetables and fruit for Piggly-Wiggly and Kroger's, the main grocery stores in America's cities in 1946. They have lots of food to share. They also have many jobs, some permanent and some temporary or part-time." Amanda continued, "When the unemployed men come to town, they often come to our home. Mother will have them mow the lawn, split wood for the winter woodpile, or have them do something in the garden in exchange for a good meal with dessert and something to drink, such as iced lemonade or hot chocolate, depending on the season."

"One nice man who came to Merrysville in April introduced himself as Frank Johnson. He worked for a meal at our home. Mr. Johnson talked to Dad and told him several repairs that needed to be done at our house and property. He knew he could accomplish them."

Dad did not tell Mr. Johnson, but he asked his friend Nelson Webb, the county sheriff, to check out Mr. Johnson's background.

The sheriff in Ohio told him that Frank Johnson, his wife, and children have good reputations. He told Sheriff Webb that he could tell Dad that Frank Johnson would do a good job for him. He's honest, and I'm sure he would appreciate the opportunity to work."

"Mother and Dad talked it over. They agreed with Frank Johnson that the many needed repairs and painting of their house should be done now. Dad offered to pay Mr. Johnson, I think one hundred dollars a week, and he would eat with the family. They would provide sleeping quarters for him while he did the repair work. He asked Frank Johnson to pray about it and to let him know his decision.

Mr. Johnson was happy to say, "I don't need time to think about it. I was praying for a job with a Christian businessman before I was discharged from the Navy. I gladly accept your offer. Please call me Frank and let the kids too."

"Dad and Mother insisted that Frank eat his meals in the house with the family, not alone in the yard where most transients ate after doing yard work. Frank had tears in his eyes as he told Dad that he was overwhelmed when he saw the respect that our family shows to everyone."

"Frank reminded Dad that he was living in the Spitznaugle barn in the park and asked if Dad would allow him to stay down in the vegetable barn to sleep and spend his time off? It has water for cleaning food, a small bathroom with a shower, insulated walls, a solid roof, and a solid floor where he would sleep. He just asked for one blanket, which he felt would keep him comfortable."

"Dad laughed and told Frank that of course he would have his permission to live in the vegetable barn if he would like. To be honest with Frank, Dad said he wouldn't have the nerve to sleep in that barn. If Frank decided to live there, my parents would buy him a comfortable bed. However, although the barn is dry and clean, it is on the other side of the gardens, beehives, fruit orchards, and two blocks out of the village limits.

"There are no residences nearby in case of an emergency. The local switchboard closes at ten p.m. so he could not get help on the garden phone out there at night. Since there are no lights on the outside of the building, he would be walking on a dirt path, in a very dark area if he walked there in the evenings.

"Dad said his concern was because there are some wild wolves that live under the side of that barn where he would be sleeping. They have never bothered Dad nor any of his workers during the day, but...well... at this time, there are several babies and young wolves that have come to the edge of the barn, and even a few have stepped out, in the daylight. Sometimes we hear them howling at night." The three girls were shocked and asked if the wolves would bother the workers. Amanda said, "Dad said everyone is safe in the fields in the daylight. You don't work after dark."

"Under the other end of the barn are the cellars for keeping the vegetables and fruit for the winter. The stairway is on the inside of the barn. The wolves can't break through the cement cellar walls so he would be safe if he stayed inside.

The doors are always open during the day on that side of the barn. The barn doors are very solid and there is a good lock on the inside. Vegetables are being brought into the vegetable barn to wash in the long sinks all day long. Dad has seen mice droppings on the floor and set mouse traps in the barn.'

"Dad told Frank that he thinks it is because of the wolves that we have never been able to keep cats in, or around, that barn. They have all disappeared the day after Dad took them there. All other barns have resident cats. Dad has never made friends with the wolves. If Frank can, and he's never outside at night, he might be safe. Frank looked a little concerned."

"Dad told him that Mother thought he might prefer to use my playhouse. He told him that it's that cute little building, right behind our garage. Since all of you have been inside my playhouse, you know that even though it's small, it has a nice hide-a-bed, chair, table and lamp, footstool, bookcases, space heater, large window fan, and a floor lamp. Dad was sure we have an extra radio in the house that he could use. There is an outside light at the doorway and over the window.

"My powder room only has a toilet and sink, but Mother thought Frank could use the shower in the vegetable barn after work or in the morning if he didn't mind. He thought that was great. There are two cats who took up residence in my playhouse so there are no mice in there. There are pillows and blankets in my hide-a-bed."

"We have used it for guests in the past."

"He told Frank to feel free to look over both buildings before he made his decision."

"After Frank looked at my lovely playhouse, he asked me if I would mind if he used it. I smiled as I let him know that I was delighted that he has agreed to work for our family and let him know that he's welcomed to use the playhouse for as long as he's on the job. I told him it really is a fun place. I think he's gonna like it." All the girls said, "Of course he must like it. I love it."

When the gardens were planted, Amanda knew that she and her friends would be doing whatever work they were allowed. Amanda figured that she and Joyce would play tennis three days a week. She and Joyce would be visiting the park to do pull-ups, push-ups, and other exercises with their many friends. The school had a big contest in the first week of school. Kids had been told in May to exercise during the summer.

Amanda and her friends hoped to be able to earn all the awards when the school opened in September. Their daily workouts should show they had worked the hardest on improving their skills during the summer break. This summer there wouldn't be any time for them to be having girlfriends over for talking or playing with their dolls in her clubhouse.

"Frank did a great job doing the repairs. Afterward, he painted the beautiful twelve-year-old house and all the outbuildings. All barns that were part of the Martin Farms were done last. He did an excellent job on everything. The house and all of our buildings looked wonderful.

"By that time, it was nearly Decoration Day.

My parents talked about hiring Frank to supervise the many school students in the gardens and orchards. It would relieve Dad of the many hours he had spent in the past doing this.

"Dad knew Frank could also help where needed around their property and drive the delivery trucks when deliveries got too busy. They agreed to add him as a temporary employee for the summer if he would accept the added responsibilities for thirty dollars extra each week."

"He nearly cried when he said he would be happy to accept the offer. He would have been willing to do those jobs at the same pay, but he knew his wife would use the extra money to get caught up from the four weeks he was unemployed."

Joyce was excited as she asked if the girls would all like to help plan a big party for the evening of Thursday, May 30th. She explained that this holiday is called Decoration Day in some states; in others it is known as Memorial Day. Most all our part of Indiana still calls it Decoration Day.

Amanda told the girls, "The first Decoration Day took place on May 30, 1868, at Arlington National Cemetery where both Confederate and Union military were buried. Nearly fifty years ago, it was officially named Memorial Day. The day is for Americans to remember our military who gave their lives to keep America free. This year May 30th is on a Thursday. Everyone in the county will be in Merrysville on Thursday morning."

"The village has advertised the unveiling of the new signs at the east village limit for many weeks. Every newspaper and radio station has been inviting people for miles around to attend. There will be speeches and prizes. Dad said members of the newspaper and staff of the radio stations will be attending. In fact, the radio truck will be broadcasting live from the event for two hours." The girls were impressed and asked if their favorite announcer would be there.

Joyce updated the girls with the latest. "On next Friday, there will be a huge carnival that will be on six blocks of downtown streets. It will be there until Saturday evening after Decoration Day. The reason for such a large carnival being in town is to attract a bigger crowd for the unveiling of the sign on Thursday, May 30, 1946, Decoration/Memorial Day, and the fireworks that evening in the park." Two of the girls covered their ears, and all the girls laughed.

Joyce continued, "Since everyone is staying in town for the unveiling, all of our friends should be available on Thursday night. After all, it's going to be Decoration Day. That's only twelve days from now. We can sit around the fire in Amanda's field, roasting marshmallows and watching the fireworks at the park just a few blocks away."

Amanda asked the three friends who had joined them, "Do you think your families will be willing to bring you and stay for the hamburger, hot dog, and marshmallow roast?

Our parties always end up being a potluck. All of you know that everyone will probably bring their favorite dish. If someone cannot, our moms will bring enough for everyone." One by one, the three girls committed to make sure their families would be there.

Joyce reminded the girls, "Haven't you heard the news? Amanda's dad is treating all the students from Merrysville to banana splits this afternoon. You can eat them any time after noon."

The girls, who had just joined Amanda and Joyce, rolled their eyes, and said in unison, "Really?" Amanda smiled and continued, "Really. In addition, more good news. In a week, on Saturday, we plan to meet some of our other friends at the carnival from one to four pm. Not only do we get another free banana split, but businesses in town are providing free carnival rides during that time for local students. We are going to take advantage of the opportunity. Won't you three girls join us?"

Of course, the three girls were excited to plan to join Joyce and Amanda, especially since it was free.

Joyce spoke up, "I'm really excited because I'm going to be able to check out more of the rides at the carnival after I've eaten my banana split. Several of our friends will be meeting us there and have offered to go on the rides with me. Most of us will go on the Ferris wheel more than once. I can hardly wait to get on that Tilt-a-whirl. Since I'm going with several girls, I'll probably ride on both six or seven times."

Amanda interrupted. "As all of you know, I can't stand heights and I have motion sickness, so I've never wanted to go on the Ferris wheel." The expression on her face told everyone she was remembering past experiences. "And I can still remember last year. I was so embarrassed when I vomited on the Tilt-a-whirl; I never want that experience again. I still remember having to run home in those stinky clothes. I've talked to a lot of our friends who say they are scaredy-cats like me. We will probably ride only the merry-go-round and rides designed for young kids while Joyce is riding with our other brave friends."

The five girls quickly ran over to the big pond where they found the four boys fishing. The girls were bubbling over with enthusiasm as they shared their plans for the hamburger, hot dog, marshmallow roast, on the evening of Decoration Day. They hoped the boys would like the idea of the big party. The boys' response was a nod and resounding, "Sure."

The boys were more excited than the girls were; they were proud to be able to show them the twenty-one large fish they had already caught. Jimmy beamed as he told the girls, "This huge fish was my first catch of the day. I also landed these other two bluegills. Pretty nice, huh?" Jason spoke up, "Yesterday we sat here for six hours and not one fish touched our bait." Bob had a frown when he told the girls it was because they didn't start until about this time of day."

Abby made eye contact with each boy for a second. All the boys were proud after she gave them her sweetest smile, and declared, "The girls said you have been fishing for only four hours. You have to be the best fishermen who have ever fished in this pond."

A huge grin covered all the boys' faces since all of them had caught at least one fish. Before anyone said a word, Jason raised his hand to bring in his fishing pole. To everyone's delight, on the hook was a large-mouth bass. That fish sure gave Jason a fight, but everyone cheered when Chris put the net under the fish and Jason brought it in. Jason proudly announced, "Hey guys, that means we have 22 fish for dinner tonight." Joyce quickly shouted, "Way to go Jason!"

Joyce, Amanda, and the boys knew that the families of the four fishermen would get together that evening for a fish fry at one of their houses. It had become a tradition since the boys started fishing together. It would be the first fish fry that Jason's family would attend. Jimmy looked at his watch and said, "Hey, it's getting late. We have to deliver these fish, and then we should get home to clean up.

On their way home to eat lunch, the girls were so busy making plans that Joyce and Amanda forgot about the barn. They were going to meet their friends at 2 pm to eat their banana splits.

Jason spoke up, "I think my parents would really like to meet all of your families. Since we're the only family of color in town, they still don't have much of a social life." Bob agreed, "Our families are looking forward to welcoming them to Merrysville." That evening, Joyce and Amanda joined the four boys and their families for a fish fry over at the Butler family's large yard. Their son Chris was one of Jimmy and Bob's close friends.

Jason's family was happy to meet these friendly parents. Jason's dad Sam Hanaway was a pharmacist at the local drugstore. He worked from 9 am to 6 pm five days a week so he was happy to be able to attend the fish fry. His mother Tanya Hanaway was the new teacher of French in Jr. High and High School. She had the summer off. She told all the children that she hoped they would take French when they were in Jr. High or High School. Jimmy Martin said, "Sign me up. I have always wanted to speak another language." All others told her they would plan to do that when they were old enough.

Chris' dad worked at the local hardware. His mother was a hairdresser.

Chris and Jason's parents were surprised when the boys enthusiastically announced that they were going to church with Jimmy and Bob on Sunday. John Martin was all smiles as he looked at the boys and said, "That is great Chris and Jason." He faced their parents, and with a smile, he said, "I hope that your parents will make it a family event. Everyone in the church will welcome you." Mrs. Perkins smiled and said, "Please come."

The fish and fries were delicious. Everyone ate too much. Mr. and Mrs. Hanaway felt very welcome and after the party was over said they planned to attend church with Jason and the Butler, Martin, and Perkins families on Sunday.

Chapter Eighteen

Plans for Decoration Day

G radually, Amanda and Joyce asked Mrs. Martin what she thought about having a party Decoration Day evening. Amanda told her mom that all the kids had talked about it at the park.

The girls let her know that everyone was hoping that all their parents would agree that it would be a good opportunity for everyone to get to know all their friends from school, and their families.

Her mom thought a Decoration Day party was a wonderful idea. Amanda looked serious when she told her mom that if they invited everyone they wanted to invite, there could be at least forty kids, maybe more, and their parents. She and Joyce mentioned many of the items that some had volunteered to bring.

Betty smiled and assured the girls, "We'll have plenty. Most families bring a dish to pass, and a chair or blanket. Limbs and wood from clean-up day will make a great campfire. It will be big enough for everyone to sit around and get acquainted. Everyone should have fun eating, making homemade ice cream, and roasting hot dogs and marshmallows. We'll get a great view of the fireworks from that area." Joyce said, "Don't forget that many of the boys are going to fish as soon as they leave the City Sign event, so we may have fresh fish too."

Betty Martin smiled as she added, "I'm sure we'll need to pick up several packages of marshmallows and more ice cream to go along with everything brought by others if we are expecting sixty people. Right now, I will add those items to my grocery list for next week. Oh yes, I will buy several packages of hot dogs on Tuesday before the holiday. On Wednesday, the store might be sold out.

"I'll talk to your mom today Joyce, and your dad Amanda. Maybe we can shop at the Woolworth Five and Dime store to pick up some fun gifts to use for prizes with games. You girls try to come up with those games. Is it a deal?" Both girls smiled, and spoke at the same time, "It's a deal." All three of them were getting excited about the fun party it would be.

When the girls told Betty about the newest boy in their class, the three of them began talking about everyone getting to meet Benji Rosenbaum and his family. When the kids were thinking about who they should invite, they all hoped the party would give them the opportunity to get to know Benji better.

Benjamin Rosenbaum was a ten-year- old who lived with his parents in the new mansion, down at the south end of town.

Amanda seemed to be in deep thought when she turned toward her mother and told her, "Benji doesn't have any brothers or sisters and, at school, he always seems to be lonely. Joyce and I think it's because there are no other kids at his end of town. Most of his neighbors are retired men and women - they're old. Since the mansion was only completed three months before school was out for the summer, Benji didn't have the opportunity to make any close friends."

Mrs. Martin agreed that the party would be a great opportunity for Benji to get to know some kids now. She suggested the girls and their friends should include Benji in some of their fun days this summer. Joyce told Mrs. Martin, "We've invited him to several of our Friday evening cookouts. He always sounded interested, but he hasn't been able to come any time we invited him."

A fifteen-foot-high stone fence surrounded Benji's family's estate. There was a lovely, huge wooden gate, with ornate carvings. In the middle of the gate, there was a huge black metal letter R. It swung open into their driveway. The village road curved to the right, just in front of their gate, and the highway was only two miles away.

There were about twenty-two acres of neat real estate inside that fence. They had the only swimming pool in the village. In 1946, there were very few private helicopters, but the Rosenbaum property had a heliport.

Joyce mentioned, "Their gardener and chauffeur told my dad that he had seen some US Army helicopters land on the heliport when he was planting flowers." Amanda and her mom were impressed. Joyce was nodding her head as she added, "When the family moved into town, everyone wondered who they were. At first, there were rumors that his dad might be a gangster. They always have a lot of expensive cars and limousines coming to visit them. They usually leave their gate open, so everyone can see their mansion and the area where the chauffeurs drop off guests.

"When Mr. Andy's construction workers were building the house, one of them told my dad that they had a six-car garage and large dressing rooms built. They are attached to the other side of the large garage.

Next to the dressing rooms is their heated swimming pool. Their gardener said he lives in a lovely apartment over the garage and dressing rooms." Amanda and her mother were speechless as Joyce continued, "Many people in our church wonder why Benji's family is one of the few families in town who don't attend one of the local churches."

Betty Martin wasn't a gossip. She had never heard anything at church about the newest family in town. She told the girls, "I think I should call his mother sometime today and invite them to the cook-out on Monday, and I'll invite them to be our guests at church. Why don't you girls have a glass of orange juice, and I'll call right now while I'm thinking about it?" Amanda poured the orange juice.

Because of the boys' talk about no fish biting yesterday, and today's banana splits, the girls had walked into Amanda's room to discuss the party, and hideout possibilities. They felt good about having the hideout organized. They knew that they would take items there to make it more comfortable in the future. They ran to the window seat where Amanda kept her dolls. It was their favorite place to talk.

The thick curved cushion was very comfortable. The cushion material matched Amanda's beautiful bedspread and pillow shams that had pictures of many happy cats. The girls moved some of the dolls to the middle of the seat so they could discuss the barn.

Joyce held a lovely pink pillow in her lap as she enthusiastically shared, "I've been thinking about the barn ever since I went to bed last night." Her fingers were nervously circling a button on the pillow. "I'm pleased your mom thinks like my mother about the plan for a hideout." Joyce leaned toward Amanda to hear her question since the girls were nearly whispering.

Amanda was giggling nervously, "What if we have over a hundred people at the party?" Joyce was giggling, too, at that possibility. Discussion followed about making sure the fire would be big enough to allow everyone to heat the marshmallows and hot dogs. The possibility made them realize the entire backyard would be used. Joyce said, "We also better pray for good weather and good fishing. The boys will be disappointed if they don't catch several fish." Amanda agreed.

When Mrs. Rosenbaum answered Betty's call, Amanda's mom introduced herself, "Hello Mrs. Rosenbaum. I want to introduce myself. My name is Betty Martin. My children, Amanda and Jimmy, have told me what a fine young man your son Benjamin is. Our family would like to invite you and your family to come to a cookout we are hosting on Memorial Day, Thursday evening. It will be on our property, and the children are expecting at least sixty people. We will have a hot dog and marshmallow roast, as well as cooking chicken, hamburgers, and fish on the grills.

I think all of you will enjoy it, and it will allow you and Mr. Rosenbaum to meet all the boys and girls that your son has mentioned to you. I'm sorry that I haven't called you earlier to invite you to visit our church."

After a short conversation, Amanda's mom was smiling at the phone when Benji's mom gladly accepted the invitation to the cookout. His mother sounded so happy she was about to cry. She told Amanda's mom, "Other than children who were calling to talk to Benjamin, you are the first person from Merrysville to call here.

Thank you for calling, Betty. Not only will the three of us be there at 6 p.m., and since I love to make bagels, I'll bake all afternoon, and bring several, along with many of my homemade cream cheese spreads. If you're expecting more than sixty guests to attend, we'll need several. By the way, my name is Martha and my husband is David."

"I don't know if Benjamin has told the school children that we are Jewish and attend a Synagogue in a city several miles from Merrysville on Friday evenings. That is why Benjamin has not been able to attend any of the parties to get acquainted with the kids from school. I can tell you that on the times when Benjamin has had to refuse, he has been an unhappy camper." Both mothers laughed. "Sometimes Benjamin is shy about being Jewish."

Betty assured Mrs. Rosenbaum, "Knowing the children of our church, I'm sure they're going to be very impressed when they hear about your family being Jewish. Everyone in the church we attend have joined millions of Christians all over the world to pray for the Jewish people. I hope you know that all Christians, everywhere, are so sorry after hearing about the persecution that the Jewish people suffered during the war.

"In fact, the children in our church have been learning about the Jewish religion in Sunday School." Mrs. Martin heard a sigh of relief when Mrs. Rosenbaum responded, "Oh that is so good. I'll tell Benjamin, and I'm sure he'll be pleased." The women had a wonderful talk. Mrs. Rosenbaum was pleased to learn that she would be able to purchase her fresh fruit, vegetables, and flowers locally.

Betty Martin learned that Mr. Rosenbaum was the president of a large national well-known corporation. Mrs. Rosenbaum explained, "My husband has learned that several purchasing employees prefer to come by helicopter to our home. It's easier landing on the heliport in our side yard than it is to land at the Lafayette airport and find a taxi to get to David's office five miles from there. Getting tickets on buses and trains into this part of Indiana from Washington D.C. or other large cities is nearly impossible. Until the United States builds some decent highways, by plane or helicopter is the choice of transportation by its customers.

"I don't know if you're aware that our neighbors, George and Fern Wagner, have a landing strip for their crop-dusting planes. He has given my husband permission for his customers to land small planes there. There is a gate between the landing strip and our yard."

"My husband was promised that pilots would try to follow highways and roads. They agreed not to fly over farms and the village, but would follow roads, so they didn't bother animals or the village residents. I hope they haven't caused too much disturbance." Mrs. Martin assured her, "I have never heard a helicopter or small plane over the village, nor has anyone told me about hearing one."

The girls talked as fast as they could about many things they would like to do in the barn. As soon as they heard Mrs. Martin hang up the phone, they ran back to talk to her. They were impressed to learn that Benji was Jewish.

On Monday evening, the Martin yard was full of 10,11, and 12- year-olds. The conversation quickly returned to the possibility of the roast on the evening of Decoration Day. One of the boys suggested, "Let's have Jimmy's dad light up one of the brush piles in the big garden nearest to the house. Just last week when we were cleaning up our yards, we took a lot of limbs over to that pile." The rest of the boys, remembering clean-up day, agreed. "We can bring folding chairs or blankets to sit on." Amanda chimed in, "Everyone could pig out on hotdogs, maybe hamburgers, or fish that you boys could catch on Thursday." The boys thought catching fish on Thursday afternoon after the Sign celebration could be fun.

Jimmy suggested, "Maybe our mom could make her delicious French fries that Thursday evening." The short boy, Jason, spoke up, "Hey, my parents just got a new ice cream maker. We could take turns cranking it. Do all of you like homemade ice cream?" Their smiles and nods were affirmative.

Jimmy continued, "I'm sure that everyone else who will attend the Decoration Day party next Thursday will enjoy meeting your parents, Jason. They'll be busy after they get to know everyone. I'm sure that Dad and Mom will try to get them to bring your family to church on Sunday. Our mom makes a great salad, and Dad is working on making his salad dressing. I'm sure he'd like to have our opinions on the taste." Everyone added their suggestions for a fun Thursday evening.

Someone suggested that, if their moms and dads allowed them to, it would be neat if they could invite other friends to join them. Abby asked, "Amanda and Jimmy, does your dad still have some apples in storage?" Jimmy nodded, "I'm sure he does." Abby continued, "How many of you can bob for apples and get one, without drowning?" Everyone giggled at the thought. Another girl asked, "Do you ever roast marshmallows? Mom just bought a huge box."

One of the girls wanted to invite all their friends that were going to join them later for those delicious banana splits; then, if all our friends aren't there, we can meet them at the park."

Betty told them, "I must remember to ask your dad to contact the men who like to play their violins, guitars, and other instruments for the square and round dances. That will make this party lots of fun." Both girls thought it was a great idea and joked about whether any of the boys would be willing to learn how to dance. Betty agreed with the girls that it would be unlikely. She said, "I'll have your dad invite Mr. Andy over for dinner sometime soon."

She smiled, and then as an afterthought, suggested, "Better than have your dad do that, I think you two girls should invite him to the Decoration Day evening party when you see him at church tomorrow. It would give everyone a chance to meet him and the opportunity to talk about tennis. What do you girls think?"

Joyce was nearly jumping up and down with anticipation. She quickly answered, "I love it. Amanda and I will make sure to find him as soon as we get into the church building."

On Sunday, the girls stopped Mr. Andy in the hallway. Amanda was the first to tell him how much the kids enjoyed hearing him talk about the barn and the park. "Mr. Andy, Mother suggested that we'd enjoy it if you'd be our guest at the Decoration Day/Memorial Day evening party in our garden. There'll be about sixty of our best friends there." He was pleased to accept. Joyce spoke up, "Mom and Mrs. Martin said you don't have to bring anything except a folding chair." He smiled and told her, "I can do that." Amanda let out a whistle, and shouted, "That's great." Joyce broke into a wide smile that lit up her face and showed off her dimples.

A few minutes later, the boys ran up to him and invited him to the Decoration Day party. Not mentioning the girls' prior invitation, he told them that he would love to join them. Bob asked him, "Would you tell us more about the history of Merrysville at the sign unveiling? Also, do you think that you could come to school in September, and tell all the schools about their village?"

"On behalf of all my friends, I wanted to apologize for leaving the barn in such a hurry on Friday morning. We appreciated everything you told us. We never caught a fish after we left the barn on Friday."

"However, on Saturday morning we caught a lot of fish." Jason spoke up, "We shared them with all our families at a fish fry last night, and our families permitted us to go fishing after the Sign celebration. All the fish we catch can be eaten at the party on Thursday evening."

Mr. Andy patted all the boys on their shoulders as he told them, "All of you have to be so proud that every one of you was able to catch something, and then to be able to share them with your families.

I am also glad to see you boys were able to make it here today. I hope to see all of you next Sunday, then I'll see you the next week on Thursday, May 30th."

Jason couldn't hold his excitement any longer.

He smiled as he blurted out, "After we quit fishing, I pulled in my line and there was a big-mouth bass on the hook.

He was big." Mr. Andy smiled and said, "Way to go Jason." As the boys left to go to Sunday School class, all of them were wearing a broad, pleased smile. Within an hour, Mr. Andy welcomed Jason's and Chris' parents to the church services.

After Sunday evening services, many kids showed up at Joyce and Bob's yard. Their mother brought out a big dish of cookies and ice cream cones. She placed them on the big round umbrella table. When she came back with some lemonade, the ice cream cones were gone. The boys and girls talked to her as they ate the cookies with the lemonade.

Chapter Nineteen

Good Deed for May

Just before the holiday, the girls were talking about what good deed they should do in June. Amanda asked Joyce, "Do you remember this time last month when we were trying to decide what our good deed for May should be?" Both girls closed their eyes and remembered:

Monday morning, in the privacy of Amanda's bedroom, she and Joyce talked about what their good deed for May could be. First, they pondered anything they could do for one of the two women that their families had more-or-less adopted. They couldn't think of a thing that either widow needed.

The girls or someone else in their families had already done everything. Joyce said, "Your family or my family take them fresh food several times a week."

"Our mothers cook nice meals for the two women at least three times a week. Last week my mother washed all of Mrs. Jones' windows and curtains."

Amanda nodded, "Mother did Mrs. Brush's windows and curtains last month. Our brothers take care of both of their yards and flowers, so everything they wanted to be done is finished. You and I often give them backrubs. We certainly can't let a month go by without doing some other good deed."

After many areas of service were discussed, Amanda suggested, "All those good deeds sound admirable, but...wait, I've got an idea."

Joyce looked at Amanda as she continued, "We always do something good for someone in the village. How would you like to help me clean the grass from around my great grandparents' tombstone? We could walk the mile out to the cemetery and remove the grass on the grave that wasn't mowed when all the rest of the area was."

"Since Great Grandpa was a wounded veteran of the Civil War, Mother likes to decorate his grave before Decoration Day. We saw that the groundskeeper, John Price, or his helpers, for some reason, had left a lot of the grass near the front of the stone. It looked awful. His was the only grave we saw where they left tall grass."

"Mother was so disappointed, but we did not have any tools, and we were in a hurry, so Mother said she would try to get out there this week."

"Mother was sure it got neglected because Mr. Price was in a hurry to finish the cemetery's lawn. He usually inspected all the work done by the mowers. Mother thinks he was waiting for the arrival of many volunteers from the American Legion. Those are the people who put American flags on graves of all veterans. I guess they're probably veterans themselves." The thought puzzled Joyce, "How do they know which graves need a flag?" Amanda was surprised by the question. "I really don't know. There needs to be a list somewhere, I guess. We can ask Mr. Price when we see him downtown."

"The volunteers put the flags on the graves so that the patriotic crowd that always shows up on Decoration Day, Flag Day, Veterans Day, and the Fourth of July, or the days before, will know who has served in the military to protect this country. You'll be surprised when you see how many veterans we have in our cemetery, Joyce."

Joyce had a big smile on her face as she admitted, "I've never been to any cemetery, and I don't have anyone buried in the local one, but I'd be happy to go with you to make the graves look nice. I think your mom will be pleased that you want to help her by doing it. Do you think I should have Mother make us some cookies and a lunch so we could picnic afterward?"

"Wow! That sounds like a great idea Joyce." Joyce and Amanda loved the beautiful and delicious picnics that Mrs. Perkins created.

Both of their mothers were convinced that their daughters were the most considerate of anyone their age when they heard their plan.

Joyce's mother remarked, "Betty, it sounds like Amanda recognized your hurt feelings about your grandfather's grave being neglected by the mowers." Betty admitted that she was disappointed because her family's grave was the only one neglected.

Joyce's mother reminded her that her family's graves were in a graveyard, south of Indianapolis. Iris Belle remembered that her parents showed them a lovely headstone with their names engraved on it several years ago. When she asked Joyce if she remembered, she shook her head no. Joyce asked, "Mother, what's the difference between a graveyard and a cemetery?"

Her mother laughed and acknowledged, "I'm not sure there is a difference, but I've heard that a graveyard is typically connected to a churchyard, whereas a cemetery is typically a burial site that stands alone, not connected to a church. Do you remember the Sunday that we went to church with your grandma and grandpa last Easter? The gravestones in the yard behind the church are for people buried there. That is called a graveyard. If the one here isn't next to a church, then it's probably called a cemetery." Betty looked surprised when she heard the explanation and said, "I declare Iris Belle, you have the most interesting knowledge of any of my friends."

Everyone smiled.

Both mothers reminded the girls to be careful on their way to and from the cemetery. Betty offered to take the girls out to the cemetery and let them walk back, but both girls wanted to walk. Joyce's mom made a wonderful sack lunch for the girls. Both girls took their thermos jugs from their school lunch buckets and placed them in the wicker basket each was carrying. Amanda's basket also held tools for trimming the grass while Joyce had a blanket over the food and thermos in her basket.

The girls walked north on the paved road, out of the village limits for three- quarters of a mile, then turned left at Noble Corner.

Both girls suddenly felt hungry when they saw a well-mown pasture with Mr. Andy's horses grazing at the other end of the field. Amanda handed Joyce the basket while she climbed the fence, then reached for both baskets. After Joyce nearly jumped the fence, she spread out the light blanket and sat down.

Both girls were excited to see what Joyce's mother had prepared for their picnic. What a treat! She had packed eight large cookies in one container, a small bag of Red Dot potato chips for the girls to share, and two large sandwiches, filled with delicious Peter Pan peanut butter and the black raspberry jam for which she was renowned.

Two big apples were sitting under the sandwiches, letting the girls know there was no chance they would be hungry before they returned home.

Each girl took one of the chocolate chip cookies and poured a five-ounce capful of the ice-cold milk in their thermos bottles. Before they realized what they had done, the two smiling girls had consumed the eight cookies and all the milk. Joyce laughed as she patted her stomach. "Amanda, can you believe that we just finished off eight large cookies?" Both girls laughed and agreed that they could not eat another bite for now.

As an afterthought, Amanda turned to Joyce, "Let's not forget to fill the thermos containers with cold water from the pump at the cemetery. We'll want the liquid to drink with the sandwiches and chips."

When Joyce picked up the basket, she spun around and lifted it above her head as she told Amanda, "I can't believe how much lighter this basket is with the cookies and milk gone." For some reason, the thought struck Amanda as hilarious and caused her to giggle while she was getting up to leave. She laughed so hard that she could hardly climb the fence.

As Joyce was nearing the fence, Mr. Andy's horses noticed the girls, and were galloping at a fast pace to get noticed before the girls were gone. Both girls petted the horses for a few minutes and then made their escape. Amanda suggested, "Why don't we each save a few bites of our apple to feed the horses on our way home?" "What a neat idea, Amanda. Let's not forget to do it!"

The next half-mile was on a dusty gravel road.

Amanda told Joyce, "Last year there was corn planted on the land bordering three sides of the cemetery. This corn belonged to the farmer that leased one of the 200-acre farms owned by Mr. Andy. Last year his corn was so much higher than any other cornfield."

Both girls were surprised to see the tall, dried corn stalks still in the fields. Most fields were plowed and planted for the season.

Joyce wondered, "How can the corn be that much taller on Mr. Andy's property than other farmers?"

Amanda told Joyce, "Last March, my dad told our family that the Farmers' Almanac reported that it was going to be an early spring. The Almanac suggested that farmers could safely plant their corn a month earlier than local farmers normally planted. Dad knew the farmer that owned the corn. He always planted with Farmers' Almanac suggestions. The weather was perfect for corn growing, and that farmer had a record-breaking harvest yield."

"This spring, just before he planned to plow those cornfields, he nearly died of a burst appendix. He was in the hospital and unable to do anything until he recovered." Amanda was proud to tell Joyce, "Dad and many other farmers have set aside four days next week to do the farmer's plowing and planting. The farmer will be able to return and supervise the farm work at that time."

It was hard for the girls to comprehend the fact that, at one time, everything in Merrysville and to the cemetery had belonged to Mr. Andy. That changed when he sold much of the farm and building lots and gave the park and ponds to the village.

This was a beautiful cemetery. Nearly every family's grave plat was surrounded by lovely flowering bushes, shrubbery, many flowers planted by caring families, and beautiful grass. Mr. Price usually did a good job keeping it neat. He hired his neighbors' sons and friends to help him mow. The six push mowers were busy many hours a day for three days a week.

Mr. Price spent a large amount of his time sharpening the blades of the mowers, so the grass was as smooth as a golf course. He hoped that by next year the cemetery could afford to buy one or two riding tractors to make the job easier. Almost everyone visited graves of loved ones only on holidays or weekends. Amanda had often gone there during the week with her family but had never seen anyone except the mowers.

After they reached their destination, the girls walked past the gravel driveway with the small "Enter" sign. As they stepped onto the cement of the second entrance, they were on the wide driveway at the center of the shiny black fence with pointed fence posts. Joyce's eyes opened wide, and she nearly whispered, "So this is what a cemetery looks like? It is so beautiful and quiet. It's much better than the graveyard where my grandparents will be buried, beside their church." Amanda studied Joyce's facial expression, and confirmed, "You're right. It is really peaceful."

Joyce pointed to the huge shadow cast by the front middle iron gate where they were standing. Both girls smiled. Joyce turned around and asked, "Do you mind if we just stand here for a few minutes, Amanda, while I soak up the beauty surrounding this impressive middle walkway?"

The question surprised Amanda, but she quickly replied, "Great!" The thought went through Amanda's mind that she had visited her great grandparents' grave many times, but she had never really noticed this gate.

The family usually drove their car down the gravel driveway at the "Enter" sign and parked near the graves. On the times they parked on the gravel space in front of the gate, her mother had always been the one to open the gate while the two of them talked. The only thing that had impressed Amanda before was the height of the "ENTRANCE" sign that loomed above the middle opening.

Below that sign were thin black metal letters identifying it as "Merrysville Cemetery." Joyce pointed a finger at the two halves of the gate.

Amanda noticed for the first time that, when closed, the two sides stood ten feet high and twenty-four feet wide, with impressive scenery, and a center closure that was a choir of angels. All quite lovely! The girls figured it was meant to represent Heaven. Amanda wondered why, in the past, she had never noticed the lovely iron artwork. She secretly vowed to begin noticing beauty like Joyce always did.

During holidays, the magnificent gate was kept open for people to walk into the cemetery if they chose. Most people who came to visit the graves of their loved ones thought the center drive was just an oversized walkway. Except for funerals, no one ever drove on it as far as Amanda knew. The third drive was the continuation of the first and used only to exit.

"ENTRANCE" welcomed them to come inside. With much fanfare, the girls opened the heavy gate. Laughing, they felt good as they held hands and walked under the huge sign.

Amanda was glad that Joyce was her friend. Joyce was teaching her to notice beauty. They crossed to the left side of the yard and began looking around at the shapes and sizes of the few gravestones at the front of the cemetery.

There was a large area where there were no graves, so the girls sauntered over to the center drive. They continued

THE BARN THAT CROWED

down the clean cement driveway, looking on both sides, and commenting on lovely stones and many unusual epitaphs.

Two large mausoleums caught the girls' eyes.

Both mausoleums were nearly a third of the way back in the cemetery, one on each side of the long cement driveway that went from the front middle gate to the back fence, next to the groundskeeper's well-kept workshop.

One of the mausoleums had the name "SPITZNAUGLE" on the front. The other had the name "JOHNSON" on the front. The beauty of the ornate carvings on each of the mausoleums was breathtaking.

The girls took time out of their schedule to walk around each one, oohing and aah-Ing. They couldn't decide which was the loveliest. Amanda said her mother told her that the Johnson family was Mr. Andy's in-laws. He and his late wife had chosen the mausoleums for their families.

The two girls returned to the center driveway to continue their leisurely walk toward the back of the cemetery, looking at various tombstones as they walked. Joyce noticed, "Amanda, there's a pump. Should we fill the thermos containers now?" After the containers were full, one girl pumped while the other cupped her hands and drank her fill with the ice cold well water.

When Joyce read aloud some of the epitaphs, the girls could not help but laugh, wondering what the person did to deserve it. They turned right and exited the middle drive, then crossed over the third drive, getting nearer to the original cemetery, to see the oldest stone they could find.

Joyce was amazed when she discovered an old stone, so weather-beaten that she could barely read, "Rupert Spitznaugle 1802-1819."

Joyce expressed surprise that there was no epitaph, "I wonder what Rupert died from, so young. I'm going to ask Mr. Andy if he was any relation to him. If he was, I wonder why he isn't in the mausoleum."

Amanda turned around to look at the old stone, "Maybe he died of one of the fevers that killed so many people at that time."

She spun around and declared, "Why, here's Great Grandma and Grandpa's graves, next to the oldest stone we could find. I am surprised that my family and I never noticed that before. See Great Grandpa's special flag that lets everyone know that he fought for the North in the Civil War."

The girls walked around the old gravestone to the area belonging to Amanda's family. Her great grandparents were born in 1826 and 1834 and died in 1909 and 1920.

Her grandparents' graves were surrounded by shrubbery and the lilac bushes whose blossoms smelled so lovely but were nearly gone from the green bushes. For the first time, Amanda noticed that her mother's family plot was at the edge of the original cemetery.

Less than six feet behind the graves was the cornfield that surrounded the large cemetery. The tall, dried stalks were thick, and with the breeze blowing their way, the girls could hear the dryness of the old cornstalks. Joyce looked like her thoughts were a mile away before she smiled and surprised Amanda by her statement. "I just happened to think. I have never smelled dried cornstalks before. Um-m-m. It's an interesting experience. I'm glad I got the opportunity; I like it." Amanda smiled as she took the time to actually sniff the aroma. "Sniff, sniff. Um-m-m, you're right. I'd call it a unique farm smell." Both girls giggled.

Amanda put her workbag down and took out the two pairs of trimming shears. Joyce reached for the two pairs of gloves still in the bag. They were planning to have such fun trimming the overgrown grass.

When Joyce looked at the lovely stone belonging to Amanda's grandparents, she saw that the twelve-inch grass across the front of the stone took away some of its beauty. The stone was tall and very wide, with her great grandparents, two uncles, and Amanda's maternal grandparents' names and dates of birth inscribed and decorated with carvings of lovely flowers.

She couldn't help but wonder, "Why would anyone leave a strip nearly three feet deep and sixteen inches high unmown?" It didn't make sense. She and Amanda discussed possibilities.

When they looked closely between the tall grass, they were surprised, maybe shocked, to see the fur, intact, that covered the skeleton of a dead skunk. It looked like the lawnmower might have hit the tail of the skeleton. Otherwise, it appeared the skunk died of natural causes.

Both girls laughed and smiled as they had the same thoughts, "What would happen if we picked up the remains of the skunk to cut the grass? Will we share the putrid smell that probably still permeates the young man who pushed that lawnmower, or is the smell gone forever?"

Before either girl had a chance to voice her concern or solution, they quickly turned toward the gravel road as they stopped to listen to what was making the terrible racket. The big smiles on their faces suddenly changed to looks of concern.

Three old rusty trucks were coming down the gravel road about half of a mile from them. Dust was flying so thick they could hardly make out the second and third trucks. As they drew closer, the trucks appeared to have belonged to the same company at one time. All three panel trucks were a faded orange color, with the same faded green company logo on the passenger-side door. It was apparent that two of the trucks needed a new muffler.

Neither girl had ever seen a truck like them. As the trucks neared their destination, the occupants appeared to be looking toward the cemetery to be sure if they should stop.

Suddenly, the hair on both girls' arms stood straight up.

The girls huddled even closer to the large stone. For no reason, they both felt they should be afraid of whoever was in those trucks.

Joyce told Amanda in a whisper, "I can't make out the faces, but I can see that there are two men in each truck."

"I think they're slowing down."

"What if they come in here?"

Amanda answered, "If we need to, we can escape into the cornfield that is right behind us. We'll keep our heads down while we're running. With the bushes around here, they would never see us, but we'd still have to be careful." "We'd be very careful," Joyce said as she nodded. Amanda could see the fear on Joyce's face when she nearly squeaked, "Why are they following so closely to each other?"

The first truck had been less than twenty yards from the cemetery entrance when Amanda smiled and quietly said, "I hope those trucks are going to that farm on the other side of the cornfield."

Before the trucks arrived at the cemetery, an old rusty blue car came from the opposite direction and pulled into the first driveway. It only drove down the driveway about twenty feet when a man got out and stood up. The girls knelt low. Although they were quite a distance from the car, through the thick surrounding bushes, they recognized John Price's rusty blue car.

The girls sighed a sigh of relief. As the driver stood up, Joyce smiled and said, "Look, I'd recognize that dirty ole blue car anywhere, and John is wearing the brown clothes he always wears." The man quickly turned around. There was fear in her voice as she whispered, "Wait a minute Amanda, look who it is."

"It's Joe and John Price's older brother George. I recognize him, but I don't know him. Do you? Dad said he lives in another town, but he digs the graves for John."

Amanda was frightened when she admitted that her family never really knew him. She gasped, "Where is his cute little sports car? And why is he driving John's car and stopping there?"

Joyce said calmly, "Maybe someone died and he is looking at the site where he may have to dig a grave."

Joyce and Amanda felt a little calmer when they thought that was a reasonable explanation for his presence.

George did not look as old as the girls' dads, but they knew that everyone in town said he had to be older than he looked.

Neither girl knew why. Joyce thought to herself, "Why am I thinking about George's age?"

Amanda whispered to Joyce, "Do you think he's seven feet tall? He must not eat very much because he's always so skinny-looking." Joyce quietly whispered back, "No Silly, he's probably closer to six feet tall. When I have seen him in the drugstore, he was eating hamburgers or chili, and drinking strawberry milkshakes. Besides, don't a lot of your friends call you and Jimmy 'String Bean' and 'Bean Pole'?"

Both girls smiled, but within seconds, the girls noticed that George was frowning as he started looking around, first down the gravel road, then down the driveway. They both put their fingers to their mouth and said nothing.

Although they had felt safe when they recognized the blue car, they realized something was amiss when the three orange trucks stopped at the cemetery entrances. Joyce whispered, "Oh no!" The peace that the girls had felt in the cemetery was soon gone.

George yelled, quite loudly, "I want one of your trucks to drive around the exit driveway to make sure that there is no one in the cemetery." The girls thought they could hear their hearts pounding. They knew that, for some reason, there was danger in the meeting of those men.

Joyce wondered, "Why would respectable men meet in a cemetery? Why would George have a man check to see if there was anyone in the cemetery? No, it doesn't make sense." At the same time, Amanda was thinking, "There's something amiss about this meeting."

"Please God, don't let any harm come to us. If we ever needed wisdom, it's now." The girls looked around and knew they could be in danger if they were not well hidden from the driveway.

The noisy truck went slowly past their sanctuary, headed toward the other side of the driveway. The two men in that truck, Jay, and Jerry Airen, looked intently on both sides of the driveway as they drove slowly along on the gravel. The truck continued around the drive, past Mr. Price's building in back, and suddenly stopped directly across from the girls. The girls heard the passenger scream, "I think I heard someone in the cornfield across the driveway. Let me go check."

The girls felt panic as he headed toward their hiding place. Both girls were silently praying. Just then, a large raccoon came out from between the rows of corn behind them and looked around. It quickly ran toward the waiting truck.

The man jumped back into the passenger side of the cab.

The raccoon crossed the driveway in front of the gravestone, when a skunk came running out of the same cornrow and appeared to be chasing the raccoon. Both quickly ran toward the stopped truck. The driver angrily shouted,

"What are you thinking? Can't you recognize an animal when you see one?" Both girls noticed that the driver of that truck had a huge tattoo of a decorative cross on his left arm which was hanging out of the window.

He squealed his tires, with gravel spraying on both sides of the driveway, as he quickly left the area. The animals went past the back of the moving truck and disappeared into the cornfield on the opposite side from the girls.

The brake lights let the girls know that the truck had stopped more than halfway down on the driveway, beside the large Spitznaugle mausoleum. The other two rusty trucks had stopped and parked on the gravel parking spaces in front of the entranceways to the Entrance and Exit driveways. No one else could enter the cemetery.

The old blue car started up and drove down the driveway, stopping in front of the parked truck, beside the mausoleum. Four men from the other two trucks walked down the driveways and joined the men at the entrance to the mausoleum.

Amanda's whisper was nearly silent when she instructed Joyce, "Look at each man carefully, in case we have to identify the men at a later date. I have a feeling we're going to be talking to Nelson Webb, the sheriff we met at school."

The girls were confident that they had never seen these strangers in Merrysville. The girls were shocked when they saw George take a key out of his pocket and unlock the door to the mausoleum. They knew it contained many of Mr. Andy's dead relatives.

The advice and warning of the sheriff flashed through their minds. The girls looked at each other and realized they must be very quiet. Their lives probably depended on it. The girls knew the men were doing something illegal. Joyce looked over at her friend. Amanda looked pale.

They could not hear anything that the men were saying, but they began to sweat when they saw four men walk around to the back of the truck parked in the driveway. They saw them grab a large rolled-up carpet out of the back of the panel truck and carry it inside the mausoleum. It looked so heavy that Joyce whispered, "They look like that is a heavy rug. Bob and I have carried our big rugs outside to clean them. There are four men carrying that. You don't think, do you, that there could be a dead body in the rug?" Amanda's eyes were big as saucers as she nodded. She had already wondered about that possibility.

The other two men went to the back of the truck, and then followed with what appeared to be a heavy, large square box, painted black. When the men were out of the mausoleum, George locked the door, shook his shoulders for some reason, and said something to the men. All the men seemed to speak at once.

If the girls heard their conversation, they would have been even more frightened. George told the others, "This is serious business. I wish I had not shot that guy. I knew he had to die when he recognized Jay and me." Jay spoke up and said, "When Jerry and I went over to him, we planned to suffocate him. Then the County Coroner would have said he died of natural causes." One of the men said, "We still have to deal with that man's body. What is your plan for that?" Another one added, "I know we work for you George, but I didn't appreciate your telling us that this is our problem, not yours, and you didn't want to think about it until we had a plan."

Both girls had goose pimples on their arms. The sheriff's words, "If they commit one crime, they'll kill anyone that could expose them," echoed off the gravestones.

There was fear in the voice of one of the six who probably said what was on the minds of the six brothers, "It makes me feel like I don't want any of us Airen brothers to be a part of this once we get rid of everything we've stolen. I hope you don't think you'll have to kill us if we don't want to do this anymore."

The tall man sounded confident when he calmly told them, "Of course not. Just be calm. It's going to work out okay for us.

Mrs. Jennson called my brother last night to let him know that her husband is in the Lafayette hospital and the doctor told her that he would be dying in the next two or three days. He suggested she should start making funeral arrangements.

"Mrs. Jennson told John she had made plans for the funeral home. They told her that they would notify the American Legion so that there would be the military salute. She would have to take care of having the grave dug by the gravediggers. John asked me if I would be available to dig the hole, open and close the grave, and prepare it afterward. Of course, I agreed and told him how much I thought of Mr. Jennson."

"He is a nice man and has always been polite to my brothers and me." The other six men admitted they had never heard of him since they didn't live in this area.

One Airen brother asked, "What will your brothers say if they find that man's body? I've heard they are respectable men."

"They are respectable, but they will never need to know." George continued, "What I will do when Mr. Jennson dies, is use the ditch digger to dig three feet deeper than the casket holder will be set. I'll call four of you to help me get the body moved from the mausoleum and into the hole. Is that a plan? We'll throw the man's body in the deep grave and cover him with dirt. I'll stomp the dirt to the right depth, and no one will be the wiser." He could see the relief on their faces, and every man agreed to help if he was needed.

Jay offered to bring three of his brothers so they could have only one vehicle in the cemetery. That pleased everyone. The men were sternly warned, "Don't tell even one person. It'll go like clockwork, and by this time next week, we can laugh about it."

That brought a big smile to the six Airen brothers. George laughed and said, "That's better." Everyone got back into their vehicles and returned down the road.

When all four vehicles were out of sight, the girls were crying, and still spoke in whispers. They were so nervous that they were talking at the same time.

"How did George get a key to the mausoleum? Why did he drive John's car? I thought they would never leave."

"Me too. I wonder what they were talking about. Do you think John or Joe Price knows about this?"

"What road should we use to go home?"

"Isn't this the day that Mrs. Jones' yard gets mowed by John Price?"

"We can't be seen on the main road."

Both girls were visibly trembling from the event they had just witnessed. They quickly put their tools and gloves back into the bag and stood up. Amanda's voice was shaky as she spoke, "I'm so glad that we had not cut any of the grass. Oh, what if we had touched the skunk and it smelled? Maybe the skunk we saw was related to the dead skunk. If Mr. Price knows anything about this, when he mowed again, he might have noticed that someone had been here. We can never ask him about how graves of the servicemen are identified."

The statement seemed insignificant to Joyce at a time like this, but knowing Amanda was as nervous as she was, she silently nodded. They were so frightened they did not know what to do next.

They stood looking around and not saying a word.

Both looked at the large cornfield behind them and decided to walk to the end of the row, praying on the way. The large leaves of the dried corn plants felt sharp and were irritating the girls as they swiftly made their way to the end.

Both girls were trying to be brave for each other but sweat and tears were mixed as they walked, holding hands, to the unknown exit. Twice they stopped and cried on each other's shoulders. They needed to remember if there was another way into the village, avoiding the yard where Mr. Price was mowing.

By the time they were safely near their homes, they had decided that the sheriff's office had to be informed of the crime they were certain they had witnessed.

For sure they should not tell anything to the town marshal. Unfortunately, the town marshal was Mr. Price's brother, Joe. John, his brother who was the official cemetery director, was a bachelor who owned a small house near Joe's. John attended their church with Joe and his family. They didn't know if their brother George had ever been in a church.

Joyce was laughing nervously when she squeaked out, "Those poor horses aren't getting our apples today." Amanda's nerves reached their limit, and she couldn't help but laugh as she agreed, "You can say that again." Neither girl felt hungry.

When the girls walked into Amanda's house, her mother was shocked to see that their arms and legs were bloody, and they were quite shaken. She wisely said, "I'm going to call your mother, Joyce. We both need to hear this." Mrs. Perkins came over immediately. She and Betty gently cleaned the blood off their daughter's skin.

They were putting salve on their daughters' wounds while the girls were in tears and related their experience to their mothers. They agreed that the sheriff needed to know about this immediately. Mrs. Martin talked to the sheriff for a few minutes, and then told him that she was going to have him talk to Amanda.

Amanda began to tell him what the girls saw, "We were behind Great Grandma and Grandpa's large tombstone when we heard noisy trucks driving down the gravel road. When they were close enough that we could see where the noise was coming from, three old, faded orange trucks were coming toward the cemetery."

Joyce interrupted, "Don't forget to tell him that they were panel trucks, and two of them didn't have a muffler." Amanda shared that information with the sheriff, and continued, "Before the trucks came to the cemetery, we saw Mr. Price, George, the older brother of Joe, the town marshal, and John, the groundskeeper, drive into the driveway, and get out of John's car. He was wearing a brown shirt and pants, and a hat that he and John always wear when they work at the cemetery. Then the trucks stopped at the three driveways. Mr.

Price had the driver of one of the trucks to drive around the gravel driveway to see if anyone else was in there."

By this time, Amanda was crying. Joyce picked up the phone, and continued sharing the information, "We crouched down and leaned against the tombstone. It's a very big tombstone. There were lots of shrubbery and lilac bushes all around us, so they couldn't see us. Actually, a raccoon and a skunk saved our lives." Joyce told everything about their fear before the raccoon came out of the cornfield and headed toward the truck.

Joyce continued, "Four men carried out a long rug that had something rolled in it, and a big black box that seemed to be heavy. They put everything in a mausoleum marked 'Spitznaugle' because Mr. Price had unlocked that door. When they came out, Mr. Price locked the door, they talked for quite a while – we thought they'd never stop talking - and they got back into the trucks and car and left."

Amanda grabbed the phone and told the sheriff, "It's a long way out to that cemetery. To get home, we walked through cornfields and back alleys to avoid being noticed. The corn cut our legs and arms, but we kept going."

After the girls told him everything they had seen, the sheriff spoke with a very firm voice, "I am going to report that the information came from an anonymous informer." The sheriff instructed them to tell no one else, especially their brothers or friends. He asked if there was anyone else in town that had a key to the mausoleum. Amanda told him, "I'm sure that Mr. Spitznaugle must have one. After all, both mausoleums hold his family members."

The sheriff agreed to follow up with Mr. Spitznaugle and reminded them once more not to let anyone else know what they saw or their lives might be in imminent danger. Joyce was crying when she told the sheriff, "Both of us remembered that you told us that if someone has committed a crime once, they'd kill to not be caught."

The sheriff told her in a kind voice, "You two girls are very, very smart. It probably saved your lives."

The sheriff talked to Mrs. Martin again, and urged her, "I can't stress enough the importance to convince the girls of the seriousness of what they witnessed. I have already written "Anonymous" on my report. None of my employees will ever know it was you who called. I can promise you that Mr. Spitznaugle, your husbands, nor anyone else will ever be told of my source of information."

The girls promised the sheriff and their mothers that they would tell no one, and they would never again walk out to the cemetery alone. The girls felt calm after their arms and legs quit hurting. Amanda reminded Joyce that the lunch was still in the container.

When Betty hung the phone on its cradle, Iris Belle spoke up and said, "I have a concern. Joyce's dad has invited several of his business associates and their wives to a dinner party tonight at our house. As you recall, Joyce, you and your brother had planned to come over here to spend the night.

If I cancel it, I will have to share with your father and brother why our plans have changed. What do you think I should do?"

Both girls felt comfortable continuing with the previous plans. Betty promised to be there for the girls if they needed to talk and would plan something special for the four kids. By this time, the girls calmed down and had eaten the lunch that Iris Belle had prepared for their outing. Joyce said, "Amanda, I feel safe with you and your mom.

Do you feel like having me stay overnight?" Amanda smiled and said, "I'll tell you how I feel. I'll feel better if you do stay overnight."

As the girls finished the last bite of their apples, the mothers looked at them strangely when they raised their apple cores, laughed, and said in unison, "Poor horses!" They excused themselves and went into Amanda's room, where they were soon sound asleep. In a few minutes, Iris Belle came back to bring two pairs of summer slacks and long sleeve blouses for Joyce. Both girls wore their lightest summer slacks and long sleeve shirts for over two weeks while scars on their arms and legs healed.

That evening, the kids had some friends over to play hide-n-seek. Fortunately, it had cooled down, so the girls looked dressed for the weather. The boys and girls were talking about the fun time they were having this year since they were getting paid to help in the gardens. They knew this was going to be the best year of their lives.

That was the furthest thing from the minds of Joyce and Amanda.

When the girls were hiding, they were drawn toward the bushes behind the Building and Loan. They were surprised when they heard the members discussing the three families that would be paying off their mortgages in the next three weeks.

The members had a considerable concern that the mortgagees should be warned not to tell anyone when they were going to pay off their mortgages. The manager promised to have a serious talk with them.

The girls ran back to play with their friends. Amanda's voice sounded sincere when she said, "Joyce we have to help the Building and Loan to solve this mystery." Joyce whispered, "We've got to pray about this. We can't do it, but God can."

The boys were teasing the girls about trying to get some excitement in their lives. They told them that they were going to make a difference in the girls' lives.

Joyce couldn't help but whisper to Amanda, "If they only knew!" Both girls remembered that they could never share the exciting part of their lives with their brothers.

After they were done playing, the kids sat on the Martin family front porch, eating ice cream sundaes that Mrs. Martin brought out to them. She also brought out some of her homemade chocolate chip cookies. She was talking to the kids when the town marshal drove by. When he saw that several kids were having a party, he backed up and told Mrs. Martin how great their house looked since it had been painted. She thanked him and insisted that he get out of his car and talk to the kids while she made him a sundae.

When he asked the kids what they had been doing since their school was out, Bob told him, "We've been fishing and caught some big fish. We shared them with several friends at a cookout."

Jimmy asked Mr. Price, "What have you done this year? The only time we see you is at church. Do you have to flush the water tower more than once a year?" Mr. Price told them that he had not done anything special but clean the water tower and the fire truck.

A big smile was on his face when Joe Price was handed a delicious looking hot fudge sundae, heaped with ice cream, whipped cream and a large maraschino cherry. As he ate, he looked at the girls, and asked if they had done anything interesting.

Bob told him, "They get to work in the garden with us".

"We always try to get the girls to go fishing with us, but, if they are not working, they just want to stay home and play with dolls. They never have anything exciting in their lives." Jimmy nodded in agreement.

Both girls felt sure that Mr. Price must suspect that they knew something about his brother. He had never stopped at their home before. They smiled at him, and Joyce spoke up, "Those boys don't know what they're talking about. We are practicing pull-ups and push-ups. We know we can do more than anyone else in the grade school."

Amanda laughed as she glared at the boys, "We're also taking tennis lessons. We are going to have a tournament with our parents this fall. Mr. Andy is teaching us. The boys have not shown up for practice once." Mrs. Martin said, "Wait till school starts this fall, and you boys will see what your sisters are doing."

Mr. Price thanked Mrs. Martin for the delicious sundae and got back into his car. He turned on the key, shifted his car into first gear, and told the children, "Goodnight kids. Don't play on the roads. I've got to continue making my rounds through the village to make sure everyone is safe, then I can go home. My wife lets me put the twins to bed. Thanks again for the sundae." Betty Martin yelled, "Goodnight Joe. We'll see you on Sunday."

The girls felt weak from Mr. Price's visit, so they told Mrs. Martin and the boys goodnight. As soon as the girls were in Amanda's room with the door locked, they both started whispering nervously, "I was so scared that he was going to ask us if we had been out to the cemetery. I thought someone may have seen us coming out of the cornfield. I'm so glad Mom and the boys were out there and told him what they did about us."

Joyce agreed, "It must be a busy job for his wife to take care of the two-year-old twins when he works so many hours. I think his job must be pretty boring." Both girls started laughing and decided to get some good ole shuteye.

Neither the girls nor their mothers heard about anything being done during the following day. No one mentioned seeing the sheriff's car in town. Every time the girls saw Joe or John Price, their stomachs hurt, and they avoided going into any store where either man might be.

Both girls prayed that they would have no trouble sleeping, nor have any bad dreams. It was hard for anyone, but especially young girls, to have that kind of information without talking about it to anyone but their moms. They never told their dads or brothers. Life went on as usual. The girls went over to the barn every day to see if they could hear anything interesting, but they were disappointed when not one person got off the train that week.

What they did not know was that the sheriff had called Mr. Spitznaugle immediately after hanging up from talking with Mrs. Martin, Amanda, and Joyce. He told Mr. Spitznaugle that a call came in that someone had spotted some suspicious activity by his mausoleum.

He asked Mr. Spitznaugle to meet him and his two deputies at the cemetery, with his key to the mausoleums. When Mr. Spitznaugle opened the door to the mausoleum, he followed the sheriff and his deputies inside. Each of the four men carried a flashlight with a strong beam. They discovered the body of a man, wrapped in a rug.

When the deputy unrolled the rug, Mr. Spitznaugle surprised the sheriff when he spoke up, "Why, I've met that man before.

It was at a Christian men's meeting that was held over in the village of Fetzburg. I can't remember his name though, nor where he lived."

The black wooden box contained a lot of money, a pistol, jewelry, and various valuable heavy items, apparently stolen from the man's home when he was killed. The mausoleum also contained other items that had been stolen at an earlier date, and at another site. The four men recognized most of the items were reported as stolen in the last month. An interesting fact was that nothing had been stolen in Merrysville.

No one had reported anyone missing, so the sheriff had his deputies remove the body and boxes and place them in their van. After Mr. Spitznaugle mentioned that no one had been buried in the Johnson mausoleum since his wife's uncle died twenty years ago, the three men discussed the possibility that something might be hidden there. Mr. Andy handed the sheriff his keychain, which held keys to both mausoleums.

The sheriff locked the Spitznaugle mausoleum, then the four men went around to the other side and crossed over the middle drive to the Johnson mausoleum. When they entered the mausoleum, they were flabbergasted! From wall to wall, and floor to ceiling, it was full of boxes of stolen items. One box next to the door held cash, lots of it.

The men recognized some of the items that had been reported in newspapers and on the radio as missing. That meant that some of the items must have been there for two or three months.

The sheriff contacted his office and told the dispatcher to send two armed deputies and a large truck around the back gravel roads to the Merrysville Cemetery. He told them not to go through Merrysville where they might be seen.

The sheriff asked his deputies and Mr. Andy to keep this information in the strictest of confidence. They agreed. Everyone realized that these acts had been done by dangerous people. Since they had no evidence to make an arrest, they needed to catch someone. They knew that the men had murdered once and would be willing to kill again to protect their identities. The sheriff and his men were concerned that one of the robbers might come while they were loading everything onto their truck, but they did not. Not one car or truck traveled the gravel road while they were in the cemetery.

The murdered stranger's body had been taken to the County Morgue and put into a cooler. "Unknown" on the drawer label was the only identification of the corpse inside the cooler. All boxes discovered in the mausoleums were placed in a large sixteen by sixteen feet metal wire cage and covered with black canvas cloths; the cage had a strong lock on it. The sheriff put the only key to the lock on the keychain that he carried. Nothing was reported to the media.

When the sheriff and his deputies arrived at the office, they were told that a call had come in from a woman in Fetzburg.

She and the mailman noticed that no more mail could fit in her neighbor's mailbox; his car in the driveway hadn't been moved. He hadn't been seen for a few days. The neighbor and mailman thought that he might be sick. When they went to his house, they found his door unlocked and ajar.

They pushed the door farther open to discover the drawers to his desk and the dresser were turned upside down, but Claude Hatwood was nowhere to be found.

Since Fetzburg had no constable, the neighbor called the sheriff. When the sheriff and three deputies arrived, the neighbor went into the house with them. She immediately noticed that a large, expensive Oriental rug was missing in the living room.

The examiner quickly took the bedspread and sheets down on the bed; it was full of dried blood. The neighbor screamed and started crying. She showed the sheriff a picture of the man and his deceased wife that was always sitting on a table in the living room. The sheriff learned that the owner's name was Claude Hatwood, a prominent citizen of Fetzburg, who had made his fortune in oil. His neighbor proudly pointed out that his beautiful home had been built by the Spitznaugle Builders, the best in Indiana.

Mr. Hatwood's wife and their four children had died of a fever nearly twenty years ago, and he had never remarried. He had no living relatives and had told his friends that he was leaving his entire estate to the Salvation Army.

The sheriff took the wedding picture for identification. The picture looked just like the man in the cooler. The following day, the county paper's headlines announced, "DECOMPOSED BODY FOUND IN ALLEY." The paper reported that someone had dropped off the man's decomposed body in the alley behind the sheriff's office. The coroner estimated the man had been dead for at least three days.

The man's neighbor from Fetzburg identified the body of the missing resident. She was still shaken when she left the County Morgue, but reporters from two newspapers cornered her and took her next door to have a Coke while they asked her many questions. She was so shaken that she could hardly drive home.

The newspaper reported that an anonymous witness saw an old, faded orange, noisy panel truck with no muffler, pull out of that alley just before the body was discovered at two a.m. According to the newspaper, many leads were called into the sheriff's office that day. The paper said that the sheriff's office was confident that an arrest would be made within the week.

The following day, only two deaths were reported in the Obituaries:

Claude Hatwood. There was almost a full page about a very rich man, who helped many people. He was murdered.

Jack Jennson. His obituary talked about a man from Merrysville, and the many kind and caring things he had done in his life. It told about his widow and that he had been hospitalized for several days.

There was no mention of the fury caused a short time after Jack Jennson's death when his wife called Mr. Price to have him dig her husband's grave.

Although they had butterflies in their stomachs, the mothers and daughters smiled when they read about it. They could just imagine what was being discussed among the guilty parties about which faded orange truck without a muffler stole the body, and who had the valuables?

Joyce asked, "Do you think any of them had enough courage to go out and see if the stolen items were still in the Johnson Mausoleum?" Amanda expressed her concern, "Don't you think that Mr. Andy had something to do with solving this crime?"

"Remember, we told the sheriff that he probably had the keys." Betty warned the girls, "Never mention anything to anyone, including Mr. Spitznaugle, your brothers, or girlfriends. Remember, if you do, your lives will be in danger."

The next day, the newspaper wrote about a man, Jay Airen, being shot and killed in an old orange panel truck with no muffler. His truck was parked on the gravel road near a cemetery. He was still in the driver's seat when he was discovered.

Joyce was shaking when she came running into Amanda's house, carrying the newspaper. "Amanda and Mrs. Martin, there was a man killed in one of those faded orange trucks that we saw. The description fits the man we saw driving the truck that drove around the gravel drive of the cemetery."

"The paper said he had a tattoo of a big cross on his left arm. He had his left arm leaning out the window when he spotted the raccoon. Amanda and I noticed his arm. It seemed strange for him to have a large cross on his arm yet was about to do something that we could sense was wrong. Remember, Amanda, it was the truck that held the man rolled up in the large rug?"

"The newspaper said they had interviewed the sheriff's department. The sheriff felt there was a link between the two murders. He told the reporter that he was confident that there would be several arrests made before the end of the week."

The girls weren't laughing any more.

Everyone in the county was concerned.

This was a big case.

Amanda didn't mention it to her mom, but later in the day, she called the sheriff. "Hi, this is Amanda. Everyone in Merrysville is pretty shook-up. Are you okay?" He heaved an exhausted sigh, and commented, "As you girls are already aware, it's a hard life when you're fighting crime."

He told Amanda that one of the men the girls had seen at the cemetery had come into his office and told him everything that the men had done. The man told him, "My name is Jerry Airen. I'm here today because I know that I might be killed next if I go home."

"I always rode in the truck with my older brother Jay, the man who was just killed. I want to tell you everywhere we robbed. You also need to know that it was George Price, brother to Joe Price, the Merrysville marshal, who killed Mr. Hatwood, the man in the mausoleum. George panicked when Mr. Hatwood awoke during the robbery of his house."

"Mr. Hatwood recognized Joe's brother, George Price, who helped the groundskeeper, John Price, as well as my brother who was just murdered."

"I figured that if George could kill Mr. Hatwood, he must have killed my brother, and I knew that my brothers or I would be his next victim."

The sheriff expressed remorse that he had not arrested George Price the day of the murder so the second man would not have been killed. He knew he could not have done that without revealing his source and having the girls to testify at the trial. He also had promised Mr. Spitznaugle that he would not be involved."

He suggested they might want to listen to the radio after they hung up and read the evening paper.

That day, the newspaper put out two editions. Except for the day the war was over, this was their first Extra in twelve years.

The radio announcers were having a grand time praising the outstanding sheriff's department. The announcers were proud that these serious crimes were so quickly solved.

The robber Jerry Airen, who confessed, was put in a private cell in the County Jail, for his safety. The sheriff arrested the four brothers who were in the other two orange trucks, as well as George Price. All the brothers told the same story about George Price being the murderer, and swore they only assisted in the robberies. Everything they participated in was a part of George's long-range plan.

When George Price was arrested, he sounded convincing that he didn't know anything about the robberies. When the sheriff told him about the other five men telling the same story, although they were questioned separately, his face grew red with rage.

He called them traitors. He asked the sheriff, "What kind of loyalty is that?"

"I only killed the first man because he could identify Jay and me. I had never killed anyone before that. Never!"

"The traitor."

The sheriff said, "When I asked George why he had murdered the driver of the orange truck, he never denied it, but he screamed at me, 'I killed Jay because I knew that he had stolen everything from the mausoleums. He was in the truck where we put the man's body after I killed him.

"After reading the paper, I recalled that one evening I had to go to work early. I gave the dead man the keys to the mausoleums. He and his brothers used the key to store some things they had just robbed. I wasn't even with them during that robbery."

"When I checked the mausoleums and found them empty, it wasn't hard for me to figure out that the man had a second key made before he returned the keys. I know he and his brothers sold everything and didn't cut me in. Traitors, that's what they are, and I was the one with the perfect plan that allowed us to collect everything."

Amanda whistled her loudest whistle, and simply said, "Wow. It's hard for me to think like that." The sheriff was quick to tell Amanda, "Me, too, Amanda. You and Joyce do not need to worry. I did not make any comment to George. You and Joyce solved this crime, and I'm sorry, but we can never give you the credit." Amanda let the sheriff know that neither she nor Joyce ever wanted any credit. They never wanted anyone to know about their part in helping the Sheriff's Department.

The sheriff told Amanda that Joe and John Price were shocked when they heard the news on the radio. "When they called the sheriff's office, I told them that George had told me he never wanted to see either of them. They came down to the jail, but he refused to see them." Amanda knew then that Joe didn't know anything about the crimes when he stopped and ate the hot fudge sundae. She felt good about that.

The radio announcer and the local newspaper reporter were together at the jail to interview George Price. They both reported that George told them that he felt betrayed. He felt like he was the victim. Mr. Hatwood was only killed because he yelled that he recognized both George and Jay Airen, the other man George had just murdered. Both media employees reported that he showed no remorse for either murder, only anger that he was caught.

Both media reports quoted George when he threatened to kill all five of the other brothers once they were in the same jail or prison. That quote was discussed state-wide on radio, by the papers, and in private homes. In a few days, it made national news.

When Joyce and Amanda were in their hideout in the barn, Joyce got Amanda's attention when she asked her, "Do we have to do two good deeds for June since we never cut the grass at the cemetery? Remember, that was supposed to be our good deed for May.

Amanda looked like she was thinking about the question, and said, "I don't think so." Both girls were relaxed enough now that they could laugh.

Chapter Twenty

And Life Goes On

A lmost every evening the kids had friends over to play "Kick-the-Can" or Hide-and-Seek. When the girls saw cars at the local Building and Loan, they hid behind the building and listened to the meeting. The management was concerned because money, that the homeowners planned to use to pay off their mortgages, was stolen from their houses during the day. Both girls felt like they needed to help the staff and sheriff to find the crook. They were praying that God would help them to discover the person. Both girls were hoping that they would help solve it by something they heard in the barn.

Amanda's and Joyce's arms and legs were nearly healed.

They had spent three hours on the tennis court three days a week. Mr. Andy was very positive about their skill on the tennis court. Four hours a day at the gardens on the three days they were not playing tennis, kept them busy.

They had moved nice pillows and two small blankets into their hideout. They had their first experience of being in the hideout when two men came. The men had tried to find work all over town. They decided to see if they could do work to get a decent meal. They planned to take another train out shortly after they ate. The girls were disappointed. They had thought they might have something exciting happen in the barn. Joyce asked Amanda if she was afraid that the barn could be boring. Amanda told her to hang in there. She reminded her that they had experienced enough excitement at the cemetery to last the summer.

They took a break and went outside to swing and talk when three of their girlfriends ran up to the girls on the swings, "Your mother told us where we could find you." The girls all laughed and started talking at once. Amanda spoke up, "It sounds like you girls have talked to a lot of our friends. How many kids are coming on Thursday?" The three girls were concerned that there might be as many as fifty kids and their families. Each of them had told the girls what they would be bringing.

Amanda and Joyce told them about all the food and prizes that their parents had bought for the party. Instruments were scheduled for the square dances. The girls talked about the games that would be played for prizes. All five girls felt like they couldn't wait three more days. One of the girls told Joyce and Amanda about what was happening downtown.

"The carnival had been running for five days and attracted thousands of people from cities and towns all around.

Also, every farmer has spent hours on the rides every day. The rides will be leaving on Saturday night after Decoration Day. The rides are making downtown very noisy. There are twice as many rides as we had last year."

On the morning before the holiday, Amanda, Joyce and their three girlfriends left Amanda's house with large, lined baskets to go berry picking along the railroad. They were surprised to see so many ripe berries in such a small area. They soon had every basket filled to the brim. They felt like they had eaten more than they were taking to Amanda's. The girls and their mothers made the berries into fifteen pies for the party tomorrow evening.

Chapter Twenty One

Welcome to Merrysville

Joyce Perkins and Amanda Martin were among more than two thousand people who were standing and staring at the dazzling pink canvas which was covering the large marble sign. Joyce Perkins and Amanda Martin scanned the entire gathering. What a beautiful Memorial Day morning! The sun behind the sign was so bright that most of the people were wearing their sunglasses.

Joyce and Amanda scanned the entire gathering.

Since everyone in town seemed to be there, no one else paid any attention to who wasn't among the crowd. There were so many visitors from neighboring towns and villages, that it was not easy to make sure they were correct in their assessment.

When someone handed the girls a beautiful colored booklet with pictures and thirty-two pages of historical information about the village of Merrysville, a big grin crossed their faces. Immediately they remembered Joyce's suggestion to Mr. Andy at the barn. Each girl carefully put her booklet under the inside flap of the three-ring binder she was carrying.

As Mr. Andy, the mayor of Merrysville, pulled off the covering of the sign, everyone gasped, then clapped when they saw the beautiful "WELCOME TO MERRYSVILLE" masterpiece. This sign was at the west entrance to the village. Additional welcome signs were installed at the other three entrances to the village. The mayor talked about the difficulty that the sign engraver had in locating beautiful, large slabs of marble necessary to make the four signs and getting them transported to their locations.

Everyone loved the design. Several months ago, the village held a contest for the best sign design. The mayor announced that Ruthie Reaves, a ninth grader in the Art class at the local high school, was the winner of the design contest. The mayor presented Ruthie with a fifty-dollar U.S. savings bond.

She and all her friends were excited that the village chose her design.

Joyce turned to Amanda and whispered, "What about the people who have to work at hospitals and restaurants in other towns? Also, what about the two families that live south of the church?" Amanda quickly identified the people absent because of their jobs. "The people near the church had children in our class."

"They left for vacations on the afternoon of the last half-day before school was out. Have you seen those two teens who live at the edge of town?" Joyce spotted them helping the women with the food. One by one, they went down the official list of residents. The girls looked at each other in astonishment as they both noticed two important residents who were nowhere in the crowd.

Last week they overheard about some money that was stolen during the day when the owners were at work. Ever since they heard that, the girls planned to help the county sheriff's department to find the person who was responsible for the robberies. They heard the village leaders planned to keep the robberies a secret because they felt it could ruin the Merrysville Planning Committee's drive to bring more companies to their fine village. The village needed more tax dollars to continue to grow.

An emcee proudly displayed a copy of the thirty-two-page booklet, "HISTORY OF MERRYSVILLE" that everyone had received today. He stated, "This lovely booklet was written and paid for by Mayor Andy Spitznaugle, in response to the suggestion of Joyce Perkins." When they heard the emcee, the girls stopped for just a second and smiled. The mayor suggested that everyone take the lovely booklets home, read them, and save them as a keepsake to give to their grandchildren in the future. Many people stopped Joyce to thank her for her suggestion.

Several speeches about the history of the village followed. Their friend, Mr. Andy, the first speaker, spoke for only three minutes. Many of the older people talked about their family having one of the first homes, built seventy-five years ago when this village was still just a huge farm. At the time that the lots sold, no one knew that in twenty-five years those houses would play an important part in the creation of the village of Merrysville, Indiana. Yes, Merrysville was officially fifty years old today. The pride of how the people worked together to develop the lovely village of today was evident in each speaker's message, often interrupted with cheers and tears.

As people in the crowd laughed and talked, no one noticed that Joyce and Amanda were looking around, and busily taking notes.

Suddenly, the girls were tapped on the shoulder. When they spun around, there stood Nelson Webb, the County Sheriff. He called them by name, "Amanda Martin and Joyce Perkins. Thank you for your recent help. It might never have happened without your help.

"I still remember the intelligent questions you asked when I visited the school just two months ago." The girls were impressed that he could remember them. They looked him in the eye and Amanda asked him point blank, "Be honest, would it be okay with you if the two of us tried to help you solve more crimes, if we happened to hear about them?"

He started to laugh but thought better about it.

Instead, he looked serious as he faced both girls and told them, "After all your recent help, and talking to you two at school, I would be very pleased if you were willing to help me." As an afterthought, he added, "I believe in you; I know you two can do it. Your questions at school let me know that you understood my explanation of the Sheriff Department's duties."

"It seemed to be beyond what your classmates could. Small details mattered to you. It sounded like several of the other students thought the sheriff's office was something out of a Wild West movie. Your observations and comments on how we solved the bank robbery were not only mature, but they were accurate. Your recent help put Merrysville on the national map."

Both girls smiled and Joyce spoke up, "Thank you. We won't tell anyone else, since they'd think we are crazy, but right now we are here, in the middle of helping some Merrysville people solve a serious crime. Of course, they don't know we are aware of it, and we can never tell them. When we do figure out how to solve it, we will call you for your help if it's okay. We don't want anyone to ever know that we had anything to do with discovering the truth."

The sheriff was flabbergasted, but thanked them, and warned them to be careful. "Remember what I told you at school. You cannot trust anyone who has committed a crime. If they think that you are going to expose them, they might be willing to kill you." Joyce quickly agreed, "We haven't forgotten, and we're being very careful. We won't tell our village marshal, or he might ruin our plan."

"I agree, I'm glad to see that you two are using wise discretion," was his response. Although Sheriff Nelson Webb, had done all the work to bring justice to the recent murders, the national news was giving Joe Price undeserved credit for it all. Just then, John Martin spotted the threesome and joined them. He and the sheriff started a conversation, so the girls excused themselves.

The sign dedication continued for the rest of the crowd. One by one, the Village leaders shared how they had placed the city limits at four miles in each direction from the businesses in the center of the village.

One commissioner said, "There is still a lot of land remaining within the limits for businesses to build."

Another commissioner proudly continued, "For a small village of only fourteen hundred residents, this community has a lot to offer newcomers to the area. You are this community. Thanks for being so special." The speeches continued for another hour.

After the speeches ended, everyone enjoyed a strawberry shortcake and ice cream. Some of the kids went back for seconds. Many of the local kids were having a lot of fun talking to each other about what they planned to do with their free time in the summer. Nearly all junior high and high school students worked for John Martin or Art Perkins. Work was not hard, and the kids only worked four to six hours a day, five days a week. It was great, getting paid to work in the gardens and, at the same time, having the best tan of anyone when school started. The school was out for three and a half months.

Jimmy spoke up and was serious as he said, "May thirtieth, nineteen forty-six is a very special time. Just think, it has been less than a year since World War II was finally over."

"World peace influences everyone in America. High school boys no longer must worry about volunteering to go to war right out of high school. I think most of the kids that graduated plan to go to college." As they laughed and talked, no one noticed that Joyce and Amanda weren't eating, but were walking around, taking notes. Amanda smiled and declared, "Enough of the investigation for today. It is time to think 'party time' so I need to get home to help Mother."

"I saw her leave earlier." Both girls headed for home.

The local teenagers were still enjoying their conversation and dessert. Jimmy hesitated, and then continued, "On the way here, most of us boys got a lump in our throat when we noticed that our village has proudly displayed a United States flag on every light post in town. As we looked at those flags, we talked about how the stars represent our forty-eight states and the stripes, the thirteen original colonies. I nearly cried when I remembered how many American men and women were fighting to defend our flag less than a year ago."

Everyone standing there looked solemn for a few minutes.

Many had tears in their eyes. Some of the girls from the Merrysville Glee Club started singing "God Bless America."

In seconds, nearly a thousand voices were joining them. When they finished "God Bless America," voices of the patriotic citizens went into, "Oh, say can you see, by the dawn's early light." By the time the last words of the "Star Spangled Banner" were sung, most of the two thousand people were crying or hugging each other.

One of the girls standing nearby smiled and said, "I'm so glad the war is over. Thoughts of college are on the minds of most of the grads. It sounds like the kids are planning to save most of their money for college tuition."

"Others already have plans for something special that they plan to do with the money they earn, like maybe buy a used car. Our Sunday School teacher was right last Sunday. We need to know that God has blessed America, and we need to thank God that we have a good future." When they looked around, they could see everyone nodding, with serious expressions on their faces. Yes, life was good in Merrysville, Indiana, on May thirtieth, nineteen hundred forty-six.

Chapter Twenty Two

Time to Plan the Fun

Immediately following the dedication dessert, the carnival, with its many rides, was very busy. Saturday would be the last day that the carnival would operate on the streets in the middle of the village. The employees of the carnival had finished setting it up last Friday.

Most of the families in the village had been enjoying it over the long weekend. Betty told the kids that on Sunday morning the carnival would be gone from downtown and being set up in another small town. On the way home, most of the kids who were going to the party that evening had stopped at the carnival for at least one ride.

From there, some boys went fishing; some girls to help their moms with the cooking; and others to help the dads as they carefully restacked the limbs and logs for the campfire that evening. The hill where they always had their campfires was high enough to be able to see all their property and the park.

The rest of the day was devoted to having enough tree limbs and logs in reserve, to have the fire they needed for a hot dog and marshmallow roasting. They wanted it to keep the area light while they played games and danced, but not so big it would burn all night. Art Perkins promised that he and Bob would help John and Jimmy to put the fire out after the last dance.

Because of the celebration and fireworks at the park, the village soon filled up with a crowd. All parking on the village streets was full. The carnival was busier than it had ever been in town. Most of the people started on the carnival rides until the food went on sale at the big tent in the park. It was only a four-block walk to the park. The carnival would be open until midnight. The crowd was big enough that the food tent and concession stands had long waiting lines. They would be busy until long after the fireworks were completed. Betty and Iris Belle were so glad that this was not their year to serve in that tent.

They recalled how busy they were last year.

Fortunately, the owners of the grocery store announced at the Village Limits Sign celebration that the store would be open for three hours after the celebration ended, and then it would be closed until Friday morning. Amanda and Joyce went to the store for last minute mustard, pickles, and other condiments needed to assure the party would be a success. Sure enough, the store closed early. After all, the store owners,

Phyllis and Mel Jones and their children had a party to attend at the Perkins and Martin Memorial Day celebration. Phyllis Jones' brother Ellis Sandlin was visiting for the week.

Ellis was a famous singer from Las Vegas and New York. He had called John Martin and offered to bring his guitar and several of his singers to lead the party attendees in some patriotic and fun songs. John Martin loved the idea. He and Betty called everyone who had confirmed that they would be a guest at the party. When the guests were told that Ellis Sandlin was coming, they were so thrilled that not one person would have missed the party.

Some families came early to help set up, and others came to choose where they wanted their chairs and blankets to be located.

The ice cream maker was already churning with lots of help from the kids. The twelve boys that went fishing showed up and cleaned the many fish they caught. Several very-large fish were among the plates of fish to be grilled.

All the people attending the party were so glad that they didn't have to fight that crowd downtown or at the park. The parking on the grass would hold everyone attending the party. They knew attendees of the fireworks would be lucky if they didn't have to park at least half a mile away from the park. The view of the fireworks from their campfire party on the hill was going to be better than if they were at the park four blocks away.

Soon, the grassy area was crowded with people having fun. After everyone pigged out on the many types of meats, tasty dishes of food, bagels, ice cream, and desserts, the music came alive.

Following a concert by Ellis Sandlin and members of his team that were traveling with him, everyone there stood, whistled, and clapped for a long time. He pointed his fingers at the school children sitting in the front on blankets and asked them to stand up and help him in leading several patriotic songs. Never had those songs been sung so enthusiastically.

He and the kids were running to the left and the right on the hill in front of the crowd of guests. They were on the grass behind the Martin house. Some kids were leading the men, others the women and others the remaining kids. What a beautiful sound. Someone said the singing could be heard at the park. When the last song was sung, people were laughing and crying from their feelings of American patriotism.

Next, Phyllis Jones, the owner of the grocery store was a great poet so she read a poem she had written for all veterans.

John Martin had everyone who was a veteran stand up. Almost every man there, and one woman, stood up. Ellis Sandlin asked everyone to salute the veterans for their service. Most everyone was crying.

The fireworks suddenly lit up the sky and explosions sounded like they were on the hill surrounding the party attendees. Many oohs and ahs were heard around the fire. Because of the location of the party, they were overwhelmed when they realized that they were sitting under the beautiful sprays of color.

The fireworks were the best that they had ever seen. Some of the fireworks looked like the American flag. Others looked like warships in a battle. Never had anyone seen a display like this one. The village spent a lot of money this year to celebrate. After all, this was a triple special night.

First, this was Memorial Day. Everyone could think of someone who had lost their life fighting to keep America free.

Second, everyone felt patriotic. The war was over nearly a year ago, and the United States had been on the winning team.

Third, Merrysville citizens were proud of their fiftieth anniversary. They had spent the morning celebrating her birth and growth into the village it had become.

After the fireworks, the remaining food was brought back outside for snacks, and the square dancing began. When the five girls were ready to taste the berry pies that they had helped Betty Martin and Iris Belle Perkins bake, they were told that the pies had been eaten long ago.

What a disappointment! The girls planned to go berry picking in the next few days to test their baking skills.

Many adults and most of the kids had never square danced before that evening. Every person there loved it. There was just the right amount of space for the squares.

The fiddlers had never sounded better. The two callers took turns calling the square dances. Occasionally the two violinists played a waltz or other slow songs for the romantic couples. No one had to sit out any of the dances. Most of the boys had chosen to go inside and play games after the fireworks were ended.

The girls and their mothers were not surprised.

Ellis Sandlin and his singers started singing "The Star-Spangled Banner." Almost immediately, everyone stood on their feet and together belted out every verse of that wonderful song. Ellis stood alone and sang a solo of "God Bless America." Everyone then joined together and sang, "Good Night, Our God is Watching Over You."

Mr. Andy said he enjoyed the evening more than any time since his wife died. He knew his family had done a good thing when they helped develop Merrysville.

Benji and Jason's parents were so happy to have gotten to know so many local people. Jason's mother said she and her husband had enjoyed meeting Jason's friends at the fish fry last week and agreed with everyone who said this one had to be the best party ever shared in Merrysville. As they left the party, one and all agreed, "We need to do this more often."

Chapter Twenty Three

After the Party

After the party was over, Frank Johnson helped John and Jimmy Martin and Art and Bob Perkins in making sure the fire was out. All the wood had burned down to thin smoldering embers at the bottom of the fire pit. The water hose quickly drowned any hint of fire. The floodlights revealed that not one piece of paper, junk, or food was left on the ground. The tables had been cleared and cleaned before the guests left. The five men were probably in bed by the time the guests had arrived home.

Joyce was spending the night with Amanda. Before they fell asleep, both girls were amazed at all the fun and undesirable excitement that they had experienced in the short time, less than a month, since they had been on summer vacation.

On their walk into Amanda's room, Joyce innocently asked the question, "Can June be as eventful in Merrysville as the month of May?"

Amanda's only answer was her cute, nervous, little giggle and, "We'll see."

The End

Printed in the USA
CPSIA information can be obtained
at www.ICGtesting.com
LVHW090101230824
789057LV00034B/316

9 781957 209012